The Stowaway On The Titanic

The Stowaway On The Titanic

Corinne Brown

Edited by,
Prof. Eugene R. Shaw, PhD.

iUniverse, Inc.
New York Lincoln Shanghai

The Stowaway On The Titanic

iUniverse books may be ordered through booksellers or by contacting:

iUniverse
2021 Pine Lake Road, Suite 100
Lincoln, NE 68512
www.iuniverse.com
1-800-Authors (1-800-288-4677)

ISBN: 0-595-33154-8 (pbk)
ISBN: 0-595-66754-6 (cloth)

Printed in the United States of America

Dedicated to individuals working to create a safe world
where we can live in harmony and peace.

Contents

HARLEM, NEW YORK

Friday, November 27, 1998

"Grandpa Leroy, don't tell them I'm in here!" My twelve-year-old great-grandson, Leroy Clark IV, ducked behind my reclining leather armchair. "*Pleaassssel*"

"Why?" I asked, amused by his childish behavior.

"They want to take me shopping."

"When I was young, I was very grateful if someone wanted to take me shopping."

The boy groaned. "Are you going to give your Thanksgiving speech again?"

Before I could respond, Adassa, my seventy-year-old daughter, entered the family room. "Dad!" She yelled at me as if I were deaf.

I decided to ignore her.

"Dad," she repeated, "is young Leroy in here?"

I closed the law book that rested on my lap, removed my thick eyeglasses, and made a big production of clearing my throat, but I said nothing.

"Dad," she said sternly.

"Yes, Adassa?"

Before she could respond, a loud crash came from behind me.

My great-grandson jumped to his feet and shouted, "I didn't mean to do it, Grandpa Leroy! I'm sorry." He looked at his grand-aunt. "I didn't mean to break the vase!"

"Clean it up," Adassa snapped. "And be ready to leave in ten minutes."

"He wants to stay with me," I countered.

"What are you going to do with him?"

I was irritated by her snippety tone of voice. Although I was old, I was useful. I still practiced law, and I walked in Central Park every day. I would still be driving if my know-it-all son-in-law, Dr. Mark Barclay II, would let me.

I gave my daughter the same intense look that always made the people I cross-examined in a courtroom do whatever I asked of them. "I raised five children," I growled, "and I have twelve grandchildren and fourteen great-grandchildren. I'm sure that I can find something to interest young Leroy."

My daughter acted as if I had said nothing. She reached for the medical kit and proceeded to change the bandage on my ankle. One fall down the stairs, and now my family was treating me like I was helpless. What they didn't understand—what I had never told them—was that as a child, I had survived worse.

"Did you take your pills?" Adassa asked.

"Yes," I lied.

She checked my pulse. "Are you positive you'll be okay?"

"Positive!" young Leroy responded before I could.

Adassa hesitated. She stared at me, then looked at her smiling grandnephew who was nodding his head. "Okay," she muttered, and kissed my forehead. She kissed young Leroy, too. "Leftover turkey, greens, rice and peas, pumpkin pie and sweet potato pie are in the fridge." She turned and walked out the door.

"Thanks, Grandpa Leroy." The boy grinned. "Can we watch a movie?" He dropped the last pieces of the broken vase into a wastebasket.

"Which one?"

"*Titanic.*"

"No." My tone of voice was harsher than I meant it to be.

"*Pleaasssse*, Grandpa. It's a great movie. The ship hit an iceberg and split in two." He moved his hands in an exaggerated manner to demonstrate the action.

"I know," I grunted. "I was there."

LONDON, ENGLAND

The memories of my childhood were still vivid and painful. I was born at the beginning of the twentieth century, a time of great progress—a gilded age. I was plain Leroy then, an orphan without a last name.

School was my only joy. Miss Owen, my teacher, encouraged me to read and learn all that I could. My lessons, however, were often interrupted by the jobs the master of the orphanage forced me to do.

My life changed when I met Mark Barclay in the spring of 1912. He had no friends, because the boys did not want to be around someone who cried in public. Mark's parents had died in a horrible theater fire. He had cried for most of the three weeks he had been at the orphanage

Mark was an inch taller than me, and his shoulders were broader than mine. He had unruly, red hair and big, round cheeks that were full of freckles.

Our friendship started in the dingy library at the orphanage. Mark was sitting alone at the back of the room, staring at a blank page of a notebook for almost an hour. His face was tear-stained, and his lips drooped at the corners. I felt very sorry for him, so I stopped reading the novel I was enjoying and asked him if he wanted to play.

He didn't answer.

"You'll have fun," I promised.

He wiped his runny nose with the back of his right hand, and then nodded his head as he wiped his hand on his blue shirt.

"Let's race to the backyard," I suggested.

He accepted the challenge, and to my great surprise, he won. We climbed the back wall and ran across the grounds of the local market. We passed the music hall, a church, the race-track, and a strawberry jam factory before dashing across a gravel road to enter a park.

I showed him all of my favorite spots. When darkness fell, I was ready to go back, but Mark wanted to stay and look at the stars. He taught me some of their names.

We returned to the orphanage as the lights from the candles were being put out. Mark ran down a wide hallway to get to his room, while I tiptoed along a narrower hallway to reach the dormitory where I slept with nineteen boys.

"Ah!" I gasped.

Mr. Wardles, the master of the orphanage, startled me. He was standing by my bed with a candle in his hand. When the candlelight flickered, the ugly mole on his pudgy nose appeared to be purple, then green, then purple again.

"Leeerrroooooy!" he snorted. "Get all of your things. You're going to sleep in the coal shed."

"But..."

"Now!" he barked.

I picked up the ragged brown bag that I took to school. Then I reached under my mattress, pulled out my treasure box and put it in the bag.

"Get out of here!" Mr. Wardles snapped.

I ran out the door.

The old wooden shed looked scary in the moonlight. I was afraid to enter it, but I had no other place to go. The unlocked door creaked as I opened it.

"Is anybody in here?" I asked, peeking inside. The shuffling of my shoes on the dirt floor broke the eerie silence. "Rats!" I screamed when a small animal scurried across my feet. "I hate rats."

There were no windows, so I kept the door open to let in the moonlight. I raised my right hand above my head to examine a large hole in the ceiling. "Yikes!" Dust and cobwebs fell on my face.

This place is creepy, I thought as I collapsed on the floor. I was scared, cold, and very tired. I clutched my treasure box to my chest and fell into a deep sleep.

The next morning, I woke up early and went straight to school. Mark was not there. I delivered newspapers in the afternoon and didn't return to the orphanage until it was time for the evening meal.

As I entered the dining hall, Mark greeted me with a broad smile. "I'm going to America," he announced.

"Why?" I asked as we took our seats at a table and reached for chunks of bread.

"I have an aunt who lives in New York. She's going to adopt me."

"I wish someone would adopt me," I responded in a voice that cracked. Suddenly, I was overwhelmed with feelings of loneliness and hopelessness.

"Maybe my aunt can help. Why don't you come with me?"

"How? I don't have any money."

"Let me think." He frowned. Then his face brightened. "I could sneak you on the ship!"

"They'll find out."

"Don't worry, Leroy. The *Titanic* is huge. No one will notice you."

My brown eyes opened wide. "The *Titanic*!"

"It sails tomorrow. So you're coming, Leroy?"

"Yes!"

After I finished my chores, I went to the library and found a newspaper article about the great ocean liner. Everybody had been talking about it for months, but I knew very little about the ship. After I finished reading the newspaper, I picked up a book on America. I quickly turned the pages until I found the chapter on New York City. I stared at a picture of a busy street with a sign that said, "Fifth Avenue."

"Leeerrrooooooy!"

I looked up to see the old master standing in the doorway.

His steel-blue eyes blazed with anger. "Put out that light!"

"I'm reading!" I yelled.

He walked toward me. As he spoke, stinky breath blasted from his big mouth. "Stop!"

"But…"

"But nothing." He slapped his hand on my table, and the oil lamp fell on its side.

I reached for the lamp before the flame touched my book.

"Look what you did!" Mr. Wardles' voice thundered as I placed the lamp on the windowsill behind my chair. "You almost set the place on fire."

I opened my mouth to argue, but he cut my words short. "Go to the shed now!" he ordered.

I picked up my book and defiantly turned a page.

"You need discipline." Mr. Wardles pulled the book out of my hand. "Tomorrow morning, you start working in the silk mill."

"What about school?"

He tossed the book on a shelf. "Forget about school."

"But I want to be a lawyer!" I shouted, jumping to my feet.

His growling voice spat hurtful words at me. "Negroes cannot be lawyers."

I was so angry. My jaw shook. Then I thought about leaving on the *Titanic* the next day. My lips curled into a smile as I said, "Goodnight, Ssirrrr."

"Get out of here!"

I hesitated.

"Leeeroooy..."

"Sir," I quickly interrupted him. "I'm going to be a lawyer."

He spat on my right shoe and gave me a scornful look. "You, who can't hold a job, want to be a lawyer. Let me see...the baker fired you, because you always burned the bread. As for the music hall..."

"That wasn't my fault," I explained for the hundredth time. "A rat ran in front of me when I was carrying a bucket of balls. I tripped, and the balls spilled on the floor. I told the performers to move. It wasn't my fault that the Russian acrobat didn't understand English."

Looking down his nose, Mr. Wardles continued with his outrageous charges against me. "You made the acrobat break his leg."

"No!" I screamed.

"Last month, you lost your job as a rat catcher, because the rats were smarter than you. And now you think you have the brains to be a lawyer."

"I do! I have the highest marks in class."

"Your classmates are idiots."

"Miss Owen said I was very intelligent."

"Miss Owen. Miss Owen!" Mr. Wardles growled. "Ever since that teacher arrived at the school, she has filled your head with crazy ideas. Well, tomorrow the mill will grind you up and show you that you and your intelligence are worth nothing."

I wanted to kick and scream and tell him he was a mean, horrible man. I wanted to punch him until he admitted he was wrong.

Mr. Wardles unbuckled his belt.

I ran to the coal shed.

I couldn't believe I was leaving the orphanage, the only home I had ever known. I was really going on the *Titanic*. Maybe I could get a new mother, too. I'd bring her something special.

I reached into my bag and took out the box. My treasure was still inside. *I'll give it to my new mother*, I thought.

I must have fallen asleep because I woke up startled when I heard a dog bark. It was very early on Wednesday morning, April 10, 1912.

I thought about the instructions Mark had given me. He was in the second room at the front of the orphanage. His room was next to Mr. Wardles, so I had to be very quiet.

A cold fog hung over the backyard as I stepped outside the shed. Wrapping my scarf around my neck, I ducked under a low-hanging branch of an oak tree and came face-to-face with an angry dog.

I dropped my bag, climbed the trunk of the tree, and pulled up the hem of my coat before his teeth could grab it. The dog barked so loudly, I was afraid it would wake everybody up.

"Shhh," I said, "Shhh. Go away." That didn't work. If I jumped to the ground, could I outrun him? No. I knew this dog well. Last week, he bit the milkman. Blood spurted out of the poor man's hand as he made a mad dash to his milk cart. I could still hear his loud screams in my ears.

"Good mornin', Larry." That was the familiar voice of my former boss. He owned the bakery on the other side of the wall.

A few minutes later, the ovens made loud crackling sounds as someone fired them up. That used to be one of my jobs when I worked at the bakery last year. I had to get up early and light the ovens by five o'clock every morning.

I panicked. Mark was leaving at 5:15 a.m. I had to get back on the ground immediately.

I took a deep breath. Then, very slowly, I started to climb down the tree trunk.

I heard a rustle below and froze in place. What was that? I looked down at the dog. He stopped barking, and his ears perked up.

A "meow" followed another rustling noise. Then, in a flash, the dog took off after a cat.

I jumped to the ground, picked up my bag, and ran to the side door. A single blow of a stone broke the rusty latch, and I entered the west wing.

Creeping down the cold, musty hallway, I turned left, side-stepped a creaky floorboard, turned left again, then, "Ah…" I stifled a scream. It was only a flying bat.

"Wooooo!" The wind made creepy sounds as it whistled down the hallway. "Wooo-Ooo-Ooo!"

My knees shook with fear, but I forced myself to be brave. I took two more steps and knocked on a door.

"Who is that?" the deep, familiar voice of Mr. Wardles growled.

Oops! How could I make such a mistake? I ran to the next door and knocked. Without waiting for an answer, I dashed inside and closed the door.

"You're late!" Mark said as he put on his overcoat.

"Mr. Wardles is awake," I whispered.

"Here, hide in Mum's old trunk." Mark opened the lid and took out a handful of clothes.

I pushed some books to a corner, then hugged my bag to my chest as I squeezed myself into the small space.

"It's a good thing you're so skinny," Mark said as he covered my bony knees with the clothes.

Suddenly, the door burst open.

Mark slammed down the cover of the trunk. I heard him draw a loud, sharp breath before he said, "Good morning, Mr. Wardles."

I shuddered when the old master asked, "Were you outside my room?"

"Yes." Mark lied without hesitating. "Can someone carry my trunk?"

"Must you carry that old thing?"

"Yes," Mark insisted. "It was my mother's."

"Very well. Mr. Edward will carry it." Mr. Wardles muttered something under his breath before saying, "Here he comes now. He'll take you to the *Titanic.*"

Peeping through a hole in the trunk, I saw the familiar, wrinkled face of Mr. Edward, a burly man who delivered potatoes to the orphanage every week. He was holding a pushcart. "I'll take care of this," he said.

I felt the trunk move.

"We're goin' in my wagon," Mr. Edward announced.

STOWING AWAY

The long, bouncy wagon ride came to a sudden stop. I heard Mark ask, "Why are we at Waterloo Station?"

Mr. Edward said, "Good morning Dr. and Mrs. Wells," before he answered the question. "You will travel with the doctor and his wife on the boat train. It will take you to Southampton where the *Titanic* is docked."

Looking through a hole in the trunk, I saw an elegant lady wearing a silk dress and a feather hat. She was standing next to a man in a wool suit.

"Why doesn't the ship come up the Thames?" Mark asked.

"Because it's an ocean liner that's too big to travel on the river," the man explained. "Your aunt is one of my favorite patients. I take care of her whenever she comes to Europe."

The lady joined the conversation. "You're a lucky boy," she said. "You're sailing on the greatest ship ever built, and you're going to America."

"I don't feel lucky, Mrs. Wells." Mark's voice cracked.

"Oh, how thoughtless of me," she whispered. "I forgot you just lost your parents. I'm so sorry."

Mark cried.

The journey to Southampton seemed to take forever. The rattling motion of the train and the smoke from the steam engine made me feel lightheaded and sick. But I was brave.

Mark was offering me a chance to have a better life, and I was determined not to mess it up. I had to find something to do for the rest of the journey.

I spent the time daydreaming about the family who might adopt me. I wondered what the father would be like. Maybe he would be a teacher. He could teach me everything I needed to learn so that I could grow up to be a lawyer. I hoped his wife was a good cook, because I loved to eat. Maybe she could sew? It'd be nice to have new clothes. And I really, really hoped they…

Dr. Wells' voice interrupted my dreams. "We're here," he announced.

Mark exclaimed, "The *Titanic* is huge!"

Looking through several holes in the old trunk, I couldn't see the ship—only people. They were speaking excitedly.

"Herr Schmidt," I heard an Englishman say boastfully, "it's larger than the *Lusitania*."

"But is it fast, Mr. Williams?"

"We'll arrive in New York ahead of schedule. Will you be staying in the city?"

"No," Schmidt responded. "I have business in Pennsylvania and Chicago. Then I'll visit my brother in Michigan."

"Oh!" a lady exclaimed in a highfalutin voice. "Our friends in Toronto will envy us when we tell them that we traveled on the *Titanic*."

"Look, lassie! Look, lad. Can you believe your eyes?" a Scotsman asked. "This is a floating city."

"It's so high!" a little girl exclaimed.

"It must have at least ten decks," Mr. Williams guessed.

"Magnifico!" exclaimed an Italian man. "Bravo! Bravo!"

The sounds were so familiar. The different accents and the excited chatter reminded me of the six months I worked at the music hall. I was the prop boy for performers who came from all over the world. Oh, how I regretted losing that job. But I was moving forward now, onto the *Titanic*.

I smiled when I saw a little boy running toward the trunk. He was about three years old. He put a finger in the hole, pulled it out, put it in again, and pulled it out again. Then he looked inside. I quickly closed my eyelids so that he wouldn't see the whites of my eyes. A few minutes passed before I opened my eyes again. I was very relieved to see that the three-year-old was now pulling on the skirt of a big girl.

"Porter," Dr. Wells said. "This trunk is going into the cargo hold."

Suddenly something covered the hole.

"No!" Mark shouted. "The trunk has to stay with me. I don't want it to get lost."

"But..."

Mark interrupted the doctor. "It's all my mother left me."

I held my breath as I waited to hear the response. If I was placed In the hold, what was I going to do for food?

"Oh hush, dear," Mrs. Wells said. "The poor child has lost so much. Let him keep the trunk with him."

There was a long pause, and then, to my relief, the doctor agreed.

"We're going this way," said a man with a raspy voice.

The trunk turned. And turned again. I started to feel dizzy. I wanted it to stop. But it continued to move, turning one way, then another.

I only was able to half-listen to a Scottish boy as he asked, "Mrs. Browning, do...know...long...is?"

"Over eight hundred and...," a lady with an American accent responded. "That's more...four...blocks...."

"Look...funnels!" the boy blurted out. "You...drive...train through one!"

Mercifully, the trunk stopped moving.

Mark asked, "Is it safe?"

"It's unsinkable." Dr. Wells' loud voice reassured me. "The *Titanic* was built by the best engineers. You'll be safe. Now let's find a steward."

"I'm your steward," an Englishman said. "Welcome to the *R.M.S. Titanic*. My name is Howard. I'll take care of you."

"I can take care of myself," Mark protested.

"That will make my job so much easier," Howard replied. "May I see your ticket?" He paused briefly. "One person for first class."

"I'm not travelin' with him," the doctor explained. "Mrs. Wells and I are leaving the ship in France. Master Mark Barclay will be traveling alone to New York City. He is Miss Helen Barclay's nephew."

"Is this *the* Miss Barclay, the wealthy heiress?"

"Yes," Dr. Wells replied. "She paid for his ticket."

"I know your aunt well," Howard said. "I looked after her when she traveled on the *Olympic*."

"The *Olympic*?" Mark sounded puzzled.

"It is the *Titanic*'s sister ship," Howard explained. "It was put into service last year. I'll take the trunk."

I felt the trunk move in a half circle.

"I'll show you to your room," Howard offered.

"If you need anything, you will find Mrs. Wells and me on the promenade," the doctor said.

Mark thanked them.

I peeked through the hole again. We were moving down a hallway and into an elevator. Foreigners surrounded us. I didn't understand a word they said.

When we moved out of the elevator, I saw a Japanese man speaking to a woman in a pink dress.

He asked, "Where are you going?"

"To my son's wedding," she answered. "I was booked to travel on the *Oceanic* next week, but the coal miners are on strike. The *Titanic* is using all the coal. So I feel very fortunate to get a stateroom on it."

"How nice for you, Madam. I'm sure you'll have a pleasant voyage."

"Here is your stateroom," Howard announced. "You share a bathroom with the next stateroom, but the ship is not full. So you'll have a private bathroom. I'll unpack your trunk."

"I can do that," Mark quickly responded.

"But it's my job. Miss Barclay would want me to…"

A bell rang.

"Are you sure you don't need me?" Howard asked.

"Yes, I'm sure."

"If you do, just ring that bell by the bed."

I relaxed when I heard the sound of a door closing.

"Leroy, you can come out now," Mark said as he lifted the lid of the trunk.

"Thank goodness. My head hurts and my muscles are cramped," I whined as I slowly rose to my feet.

"Stretch out on the bed," Mark suggested. He took my coat and hung it in a closet. "Are you hungry?"

"Very," I answered, making a great effort to move my wobbly legs.

"I'll get some food." Mark left the stateroom.

My head was spinning. I couldn't stand up straight, so I crawled onto the bed. It had the biggest, most comfortable mattress! The sheets and pillows were soft and smelled brand new.

After a few minutes of rest, my head started to feel better. I sat up and looked around. The stateroom was fit for a king. In addition to the large bed with a huge headboard, there were two padded chairs and a mahogany desk.

I slipped off the bed and stood on my feet. They were not so wobbly anymore. I walked over to the desk and took a closer look at the items placed on top of it.

A pen was next to a silver-plated inkwell. In the middle of the desk was a writing pad with the famous logo of the *White Star Line*, the British company that built the *Titanic*.

An electric lamp was at the back of the desk. I found the lamp switch and turned it on. I turned it off, and I turned it on again. The light switch worked just like the one at the music hall. I could have light whenever I wanted! Now I could read all night without worrying that a candle would burn down the room.

There were two other electric lamps. They were gold-plated and attached to the wall. There was also a gold-plated mirror and a huge dresser with a crystal dish full of candy on top. I reached for a candy and removed the silver wrapping. When I placed the candy in my mouth, the mint melted on my tongue. Oh, how delicious! I ate another candy and continued to explore my surroundings.

The ceiling was painted crimson red. The walls were covered with thick paper, and soft, red carpet cushioned my feet.

I opened a door that led to the closet and imagined having clothes to fill it up. Maybe one day I would, I thought. After all, once I reached America, anything was possible.

My heart filled with excitement as I entered the private bathroom.

A private bathroom! I'd never seen such a thing. At the orphanage, I had to take my monthly bath in the kitchen with all the other boys.

I stood in front of the porcelain sink. I could run the water as long as I wanted without Mr. Wardles screaming at me, "Turn that tap off!"

It was a very fancy sink with the name of the manufacturer—*Doulton & Co., Limited*—printed just below the gold-plated faucet. There were two taps. I turned one on. It had very cold water. The other—"Ouch!" It burned my fingers. It had hot water.

I wondered how they got the hot water in the tap. If this was how they built a stateroom, I could hardly wait to see the rest of the ship.

Mark finally returned with sandwiches, cheese, milk, and French ice cream. He bubbled with excitement. "This ship has everything!"

The wonderful smell of the food distracted me. "Let's explore it after we eat."

The ship's whistle blew three times.

"The *Titanic* is leaving!" Mark ran to the porthole and waved good-bye to the people on the dock. I didn't get up. I was busy wolfing down a sandwich.

"We're passing another ship," Mark announced. "Guess what its name is."

I didn't respond, because my mouth was full of bread.

"It's the *New York*!" he told me. "Can you believe that? We're passing a ship called *New York* as we're sailing to New York!" His laugh was cut short by a scream.

"What's wrong?" I asked.

"Stop!" Mark covered his eyes and backed away from the porthole.

"What!?" I exclaimed and ran to the porthole. Oh, no! The suction of the *Titanic* was pulling the *New York* away from the pier. "The ships are going to crash!" I yelled.

People on the dock shouted at the *Titanic* to steer the other way. But the ocean liner and the *New York* moved closer to each other. Just before a possible crash, the *Titanic* turned away from the smaller ship.

I was very relieved. "Mark, it's going to be all right."

He looked worried. "Leroy, they don't know how to steer this ship!"

Although I secretly agreed with him, I tried to be positive. "That was a silly mistake. It won't happen again."

"I hope you're right."

I hoped so, too!

"We could get off in France," he suggested.

"What?"

"We're stopping in Cherbourg, France, this evening," Mark explained. "We could leave the ship there."

"Do you think that Dr. Wells will allow you to leave the ship with him?" I asked.

Mark frowned. "How about getting off in Ireland? That's the next stop."

"No! I'm not leaving the *Titanic* until I reach America."

THE TITANIC

"Ar-r-r-rggg!" I jumped off the bed and ran to the bathroom sink.

"What's wrong?" Mark asked.

I vomited.

"Oh, no!" he wailed.

"Ar-r-r-rggg."

"Are you finished?"

I could barely speak. "My stomach feels funny."

"You must be seasick." He handed me a rag, and I used it to clean my face. "Go to bed," he urged. "The waves are rough. You'll get used to them soon."

I fell asleep and awoke several hours later to find myself alone in a dark room. My head hurt and my eyes were puffy. I must have fallen asleep again, because I woke up startled when Mark came back to the stateroom and turned on a lamp.

"I had dinner," he said. "A steward wanted me to eat in a small room with the little children and the servants, but I insisted on eating in the first-class dining saloon. Mrs. Browning took my side." Mark grinned and puffed up his chest. "She said that if I was old enough to travel alone, I was old enough to eat in the saloon. Mrs. Browning is a loud, bossy woman, but I like her." Mark's eyes opened wide and he moved his hands far apart. "You should see the saloon!" he exclaimed. "It's huge! More than one hundred feet!"

"Oh," I responded unenthusiastically.

"There were hundreds of people in there. I sat at a table with Mrs. Sanders, Mrs. Browning, and Mr. and Mrs. Hillock. We had lobster..."

At the mention of food, my stomach felt very sick. I jumped off the bed and ran to the toilet.

"Not again!" he whined.

There was very little left in my stomach to bring up. I washed my face and crawled back to bed. "Sorry, I'm not much fun."

He patted my shoulder. "Leroy, it's not your fault. Some people just get seasick. Mrs. Browning said that several passengers were so sick, they had to go to the hospital."

The ship has a hospital! *It must be truly big,* I thought.

"I can take you there," Mark offered.

"No."

"Are you sure?"

"Yes." If there was one thing I hated more than being sick, it was hospitals. The nurses always wanted you to take yucky tasting medicine. Besides, they'd find out that I was a stowaway.

I was about to drift back to sleep when he asked, "Can you make it to America?"

I raised my head off the pillow to look at his face. I wondered why he was asking me that question. Did Mark want me to get off the ship with him in Ireland? Gathering all the strength I could, I said in my most convincing voice, "I can make it!"

He grinned. "I'm going to America, too."

As he turned off the lamp, I placed my head on the pillow and smiled.

When I woke up Thursday morning, I still felt sick. I went to the bathroom, and as I was about to turn on the tap, there was a knock at the stateroom door.

I heard Howard's familiar voice say, "Good morning. I brought you breakfast."

"Thank you," Mark responded. "But that will not be necessary from now on."

I peeked around the bathroom door and saw Howard place a tray of scones, fruit, and tea on the desk. He said, "I'll be back later to make your bed."

"I can do that," Mark said.

"Master Barclay, you're an unusual first-class passenger," Howard noted. "The other passengers want me to be at their beck and call, but you won't let me do anything for you."

"I believe in taking care of myself," Mark said as a bell rang over and over again. "I think someone needs you."

"Well," Howard sounded doubtful. "If you're sure…"

"Yes."

Another bell rang. I heard Howard's heavy footsteps rushing away.

"Whew!" I exclaimed stepping back into the bedroom. "I thought he'd never leave."

"I can handle Howard." Mark's grin reassured me. "My mother was an actress. She taught me how to act."

"She taught you well," I said, flopping down on the padded chair. My skin felt prickly. I scratched my back and neck, but the prickliness continued. "Mark," I said, "I need to take a shower. How does it work?"

I followed him into the bathroom where he showed me how to turn the taps so that I had the right mixture of hot and cold water. Then he left me to enjoy my first shower, while he went to the Marconi Room to send a telegram to his aunt in New York City.

I loved the shower. It felt like rain, and I had always loved to play in the rain. But now I was getting clean instead of muddy. Although the shower felt good, it didn't help my seasickness. When I returned to the stateroom, I went back to bed.

On Friday, my sickness was worse, and the room was very cold. I tried to warm up by taking another hot shower.

"The steward brought more blankets," Mark informed me on my return to the bedroom. "Howard said the heat isn't working in parts of the ship."

"Why?" I asked, covering myself with four blankets that I pulled up to my chin.

"They're having trouble with the heating system," he explained. "Howard promised it would be fixed soon."

Saturday morning, the heat came on, and the ocean was calmer. I started to feel better that evening, but I was still too weak to stand up.

"Are you hungry?" Mark asked.

"I could eat some pastries."

He brought me a tray full of sandwiches, cake and fruits. I gobbled them up while Mark sat cross-legged on the bed and read the daily newspaper that was published by the *Titanic*.

"It's incredible," he declared. "The ship sailed 386 miles on Thursday, and 519 on Friday."

"It looks like we'll get to New York ahead of schedule," I said.

Mark frowned. "Captain Smith canceled the emergency drill that was scheduled for tomorrow morning. I wonder why he did that."

"He must think the ship is very safe," I answered. "Remember Dr. Wells said that the *Titanic* is unsinkable. I can't wait to explore it."

"You're feeling better, Leroy?"

"Much." I jumped to my feet. "Look, my food is staying down."

"Wonderful!"

"Let's go now."

"Leroy, it's after midnight. Many rooms are closed."

"I must be able to see something." Leaving the stateroom for the first time, I raced Mark down a carpeted hallway.

"Leroy, it looks like everyone went to bed. Even the smoochers."

"Well, I still want to see the ship." I approached a grand staircase. It was very wide and had a beautiful, carved wooden railing. The ceiling was a big, colored glass dome. I had never seen anything so magnificent.

"Leroy, watch this!" Mark ran to the landing, sat on the railing, put his hands in the air, and slid down to the bottom of the staircase.

I followed him, laughing all the way.

"Let's go down to the middle deck," Mark suggested.

"What's there?" I asked.

"A swimming pool."

"A swimming pool on a ship? Never heard of such a thing. Where is it?"

"I'll show you," he responded with an impish grin. Mark led me past a deserted room, down another set of stairs and turned left.

There really was a pool.

"We should go swimming tomorrow," Mark suggested.

"I can't swim."

"It's easy, Leroy. I'll teach you how to do the front and back crawl. Let me show you something else." He led me down a narrower flight of stairs.

We entered a room that smelled of fresh paint. In one corner, there were several large, white canvas bags. A broad, red stripe was near the top, and on the side were the bold printed words—**VIA ROYAL MAIL SERVICE.**

"Where are we?" I asked.

"The post office."

"The ship has its own post office?!"

"Impressive, isn't it?"

"Yeah!" I nodded my head in amazement.

Mark pulled me into another area. "This is the cargo hold."

Construction material was piled on the floor. I stepped over a rolled carpet. "What's this doing here?"

"Some of the rooms aren't finished," Mark explained. "They're still working on them." Hearing a dog, he moved in the direction of its bark.

I hesitated. Was this dog mean like that dog at the orphanage?

"Come on," Mark urged.

I was fearful as I followed him behind a huge stack of boxes, but I laughed when I saw a poodle licking Mark's hands. "She's sweet," he said, then pointed to a barking bulldog that looked as if he wanted to break out of his cage. "That one is mean!"

When I petted the head of the poodle, the bulldog seemed jealous that he wasn't getting any attention. He barked louder and threw his body against the cage. He made quite a racket, but didn't wake up a chow that was snoring in a neighboring cage.

"There's going to be a dog show on Monday," Mark said with a smile.

"I've never seen one."

"They're fun. The dogs parade, and judges decide which one is the best. One day I'm going to have a pet. But I do not want a dog. I think it would be fun to have a cat like Jenny."

"Who is Jenny?" I asked.

"The ship's cat. She just had kittens. They are in the crews' quarters. I'll take you there tomorrow."

Gleaming, red metal caught my eye. "Wow! What a car!"

"That's Mr. Carter's."

"Can we get inside?" Without waiting for an answer, I ran to the driver's door and opened it. It was a brand new Renault. The steering wheel was high, so I sat on the edge of the seat in order to see above the wheel.

Mark sat in the front passenger seat. "When I grow up," he said, "I'll own a car like this."

"So will I. We could go racing. Vroom, vroom!" We pretended I was driving the car very fast down a country road. We turned right, then made a sharp turn to the left. We narrowly missed another car. I stepped on the gas and we were traveling twenty, thirty, forty miles an hour. Screech! I slammed the brakes hard to avoid hitting a tree.

"My turn! My turn!" Mark said.

We switched places and started racing again.

"This is so much fun," he said. "Let's do it again tomorrow."

"Sure."

"I'm glad you're feeling better, Leroy. I like playing with you."

"Yeah. We always have the most fun."

We heard a squeal and jumped out of the car to investigate.

I couldn't believe my eyes. Rats were running across a stack of boxes.

"I hate rats!" I said. "They're trouble."

"They're all over the cargo hold, Leroy."

"Yikes!"

"Let's go up to the promenade," Mark suggested. "I've never seen any rats there."

"What's the promenade?"

"A place where we can play on deck. We'll take the elevator."

An elevator door was open, so we stepped inside.

"Shouldn't we wait for the elevator operator?" I asked.

"I know how this works." He pulled the lever. We started moving. "See, it's easy." The elevator passed five floors, then stopped. Mark needed my help to push the door open.

The wind was blowing on the promenade. It was cold, but I still wanted to see more of the ship. We buttoned our coats and began walking.

Mark pointed out the first-class lounge. The lights were off inside, so we moved on. Mark started to run, but I stopped at the open door of a lighted room.

A passenger was sitting inside, chewing on a cigar and reading the *Titanic*'s newspaper. He had a bushy mustache and wore fancy boots and a big, white hat. A large, brown envelope sat on a table to his right. The words—**WHITLEY RAILROAD AND INDUSTRIES**—were written in bold printed letters on the envelope. When the passenger spotted me, his mouth dropped open. He frowned and threw the paper on the floor. "What are you doing here?" he screamed at me in an unfamiliar accent.

I didn't know what I had done wrong, but it enraged this gray-haired man.

He grabbed a cane, rose slowly to his feet, and pointed an angry index finger at me. "Get out of here!"

I ran.

THE DISCOVERY

"I saw a Negro!" the passenger yelled.

"Impossible," I heard someone respond.

"Are you calling me a liar?" the passenger bellowed.

I turned around to see that the passenger was standing in the doorway. He was growling into the face of a smaller man who was wearing a steward's uniform.

"No, sir," answered the steward. "But there are no Negroes in first-class."

"Then why is he standing there?" The passenger pointed his cane in my direction.

"Boy!" the steward shouted.

I ducked into the dark, first-class lounge and ran behind some chairs. I almost knocked over a palm tree. As I dove under a table, someone turned on the lights. I shivered when I saw the shiny, black shoes of the steward run across the floor.

Tables and chairs were moved.

I crawled behind a row of chairs as I tried to circle back toward the door, but I stopped when I saw the fancy boots in the doorway.

"I can't find him," I heard the steward say. "Maybe..."

The passenger who wore the boots cut the steward off with a sarcastic remark. "Maybe you should find another job."

Someone drew a loud, sharp breath. Then the steward asked, "What am I supposed to do with the boy?"

"Throw him overboard," the passenger snapped.

I shuddered.

"I'm going to my stateroom," the passenger growled. "Let me know when we're rid of him!" He knocked his cane loudly on the floor and cursed as he limped away.

"Where could he have gone?" muttered the steward.

"What are you doing?" It was Mark's voice.

I peeked my head out from under the table and saw Mark standing by the door.

"I'm looking for a negro boy," the steward replied.

"Why?" Mark asked.

"He doesn't belong here."

"Why?"

"Because that's the way it is."

"Why?"

"Child, you ask too many questions. Now leave me alone. I'm busy."

There were sounds of more chairs and tables being moved.

I crawled out from under a table. Mark saw me and motioned for me to go into a cupboard. As I was closing the cupboard door, the steward cursed when something crashed onto the floor.

"What's that?" Mark asked.

"Bloody vase!" the steward yelled. "It cut me."

"Go to the hospital," Mark urged.

"No. I have to find that Negro."

"Maybe he went out the other door."

"Maybe he did," the steward agreed.

I heard the sounds of footsteps running.

"Leroy," Mark whispered, "are you still in here?"

"Yes."

"I'll make sure he's gone." I crawled out of the cupboard, while Mark ran outside. He returned a few minutes later. "The steward went to third class," he told me. "Let's go."

We dashed out of the lounge and ran back to the stateroom.

"Mark," I whispered as he locked the door, "where are the Negroes on the ship?"

He looked at me with a blank expression. Finally he said, "I haven't seen any."

"Why didn't you tell me this?"

"I...I..." Mark's face fell as the dumbest words I had ever heard tumbled from his trembling lips. "I didn't think anyone would notice you."

I shook my head, buried my face in my hands, groaned, and collapsed on the bed.

"Leroy," Mark's voice burst with excitement, "I *did* see a Negro in second class!"

"Can you ask him to help me?"

"I'll talk to him tomorrow," Mark promised.

I was so nervous that I had trouble falling asleep. When I did, I had an awful dream. I was in the swimming pool, and Mark was teaching me the front crawl. A steward saw us and yelled at me to get out. Unable to dry my feet, I slipped and slid as I ran down to the cargo hold. The steward chased after me. He found me hiding behind a large suitcase. When he grabbed my wet hand, I pulled away.

I ran to the car and started driving. The steward pursued me. I drove faster and faster. He was close behind. I turned a corner. There he was. I had to brake in order to avoid hitting a tree. He ran up to the driver's door and opened it!

I screamed!

"Wake up, wake up!" I felt Mark shaking me. "You're having a nightmare."

I opened my eyes and sat up in bed. Whew! Thank goodness that was only a dream!

It was noon on Sunday. Mark left the room and returned with lunch. I was starved, so I ate twice as much as he did. "This is good," I said, licking pieces of chocolate éclair from my fingers and my lips.

"You should see the amount of food in the dining room."

"Doesn't look as if I will," I sighed.

"Leroy, I'm sorry. I don't know why grownups are so stupid sometimes."

"They can be so mean."

"Dad used to say it was silly to dislike people who weren't like you. But my grandfather thought differently. So when my parents married, my grandfather cut my father out of the will because my mother's parents were working-class." Mark was so furious. His wiggling nose was as-red-as his hair. "When I grow up, I'm going to change the rules. Everyone will be treated the same."

My shoulders slumped. "So, what should I do in the meantime?"

"I'll protect you."

"Thanks," I responded halfheartedly. I didn't want to have to rely on his protection, but no other way came to mind. I guess I just had to be grateful that he was my friend.

Mark spent the afternoon searching the ship for the negro passenger. He returned to the stateroom with dinner and a report. "There is a Haitian in second class. His name is Mr. Laroche. He's with his wife and two daughters. They speak French."

"No English?!" I asked in amazement.

"I tried to talk to him, but one of his daughters was crying. Mr. Laroche and his wife took the children to their room. I don't want to disturb him now, but I'll speak with him tomorrow."

This news made me feel a little better, so I started to relax. After a delicious dinner, we took two books out of Mark's trunk. He chose *Tom Sawyer,* while I selected *Sherlock Holmes.*

Around eight o'clock, Mark looked out the porthole. "Look at all those stars!"

I joined him at the porthole. "What's that one?" I asked, pointing to a group of bright lights in the clear sky.

"I'll look it up." He took an astronomy book out of his trunk. "It's the Centaurus Constellation." We spent the next hour identifying other stars until we were interrupted by a knock.

Mark answered it while I ducked under the bed.

"Good evening," he said.

I heard a man say, "You were on the promenade last night?"

"Yes," Mark answered.

I didn't hear what the man said next, but I did hear Mark ask him to leave.

"If you see the Negro…"

Mark cut the conversation short with a firm and not-too-polite goodbye.

I came out of hiding when I heard the door close.

Mark looked worried. "Leroy, we have to be more careful."

"I know. Maybe I should get out of here."

"No! Wait until tomorrow. I'll ask Mr. Laroche for help."

"I don't want to get you or anyone else in trouble." I put on my coat, picked up my bag, and checked that my treasure box was still inside.

"What are you doing?" he asked.

"Leaving." I shoved three blankets into my bag before I opened the door.

Mark pulled me back into the room. "Wait. Stay here till we're sure everyone's asleep."

DISASTER

We left the stateroom a half-hour before midnight. Mark walked ahead of me to make sure that no one was in sight. He led me down a corridor and up a stairway. When we heard sounds of people talking and laughing, we ran back down the steps, crept along a maze of corridors, and climbed up a narrower set of stairs.

I pulled my cap down low and wrapped a scarf around my neck to protect against the bone-chilling wind. "Where are we going, Mark?"

"To the top deck. We have to be very careful because the officer's quarters are there."

"Then why are we going to that deck?"

"It has lifeboats. No one will look for you there."

When we reached the top of the stairway, we were startled by a cat chasing a fat rat.

Those awful creatures seemed to be everywhere. Oh, I prayed that there were no rats in the lifeboats.

"That is the officer's quarters," Mark whispered, pointing to rooms that were at the front of the ship. Then he faced a white wall in the middle of the deck. "That's the gymnasium. The officer's mess is behind it. Let's go this way." He moved toward a lifeboat. "What's that?" he gasped, pointing to a white mountain that suddenly appeared alongside the ship.

I felt a paralyzing dread and was unable to form an intelligent response. We stood in silence and stared.

"Iceberg!" yelled a man's voice that seemed to come from far away. "Iceberg! Iceberg!"

I had read about icebergs in school. During the spring, they break away from glaciers in the North and drift south. Many were under the surface of the Atlantic Ocean, but some jutted above the water.

We watched in amazement as the ship moved right beside the white mass. It was nearly as high as the funnels.

The ship shook slightly.

I shivered when the iceberg made a crackling sound. Pieces broke off and flew into the air. A chip fell directly into my bare right hand. It was so cold. I let it fall from my fingers. CRACK! CRACK! CRACK! It shattered into small, glistening pieces as it hit the deck.

"Watch out!" Mark yanked me away from the railing just in time to avoid being hit in the head by a chunk of ice. He looked very worried. "Do you think it damaged the ship?" he asked.

"This is the *Titanic*. Icebergs can't hurt it," I said with absolute confidence.

We watched as the iceberg disappeared into the darkness.

"The engines!" Mark gasped.

"I can't hear them."

"Exactly." His fingers dug into my right shoulder. "What's happening?"

As I opened my mouth to speak, we heard sounds coming from the officer's mess. "I can't let them find me."

"Get into that lifeboat!" Mark urged. "I'll throw them off your trail!" He headed for the officer's mess.

I climbed up to the top of the lifeboat, unlaced a corner of the canvas cover, and stepped into the boat. It was so cold, I had to put on my gloves and pull up my knee-high socks. Oh, I wished I wore long pants like men did, instead of boy's pants that only came down to my knees.

I wrapped my legs with one blanket, threw another across my shoulders, and placed the last one over my head. I felt warmer, yet I worried. There were two more days left in this voyage. Would I freeze before we arrived in New York?

Fifteen minutes passed, then Mark returned. "The *Titanic* is sinking!" he yelled.

"*It can't,*" I protested. "Dr. Wells said it was unsinkable."

"The iceberg ripped open the hull!" Mark shouted. "They're talking about lowering the lifeboats."

"What are we going to do?"

"You stay there. I'll be right back." He disappeared down the stairs.

I wondered what was happening. I heard many voices below. It sounded as if everybody was awake.

Mark reappeared within minutes with two lifejackets. He climbed into the lifeboat and handed a jacket to me. "Put this on."

I watched how Mark pulled the lifejacket over his head, drew the strings in front, and tied them. I did the same. Then we completely removed the canvas cover of the boat.

"Leroy, hide under my legs," he said as he sat down. He used the blankets to cover his legs and my body just as we heard footsteps approaching.

"Uncover the boats!" a man ordered.

"I've already removed the covers off this one," Mark noted.

"Good fellow! Now stay there. We'll get someone to take care of you."

Soon, I heard more people on deck. Then there were three booming sounds.

"What are those?" Mark asked.

"Distress rockets," a man answered. "We're trying to get ships in the area to help us."

"Darn!" a different man grumbled. "Officers get me out of bed at midnight for no reason at all. Couldn't they do this drill in the daytime?"

"It's not a drill!" snapped the first man.

"Yeah, yeah…Captain Smith should…" His words faded.

A man with a deep voice yelled, "All hands on deck!"

"Aye, aye, Sir!" responded a chorus of voices.

An Englishman shouted, "Women and children first!"

"Officer Walsh, this is *ridiculous*!" a woman yelled. "I'm not going in that small boat."

"Mrs. Crocker, the *Titanic* has a gash in its hull."

"Why are you making such a fuss?" she asked. "Officer, this ship can't sink."

"Get in the lifeboat!" Walsh barked.

"I'm a lady," Mrs. Crocker responded. "How dare you talk to me like that?"

The officer drew a loud breath, then spoke more respectfully. "Madam, please step into the boat."

"No. I'm going back to my stateroom."

Raised voices filled the air. Many were in foreign languages. "We need translators," an Irishman yelled. "Does anyone speak Yiddish or German?"

A number of people responded at the same time. It was hard to understand what they were saying.

The Irishman raised his voice again. "Does anyone speak Spanish?"

"Si," a woman responded.

"Tell them to put on their lifejackets," the Irishman ordered. "Mrs. Browning, do you need help with yours?"

"No, Mr. O'Grady," a lady responded. "But I do think Mrs. Hillock could use your assistance."

"Hold your mum's hand," said a man with a nervous, high-pitched voice. "Stay with her and be a good boy!"

An Englishwoman cried, "I can't leave my husband! I won't leave him!"

"Dear, this is only a precaution," responded an Englishman in the most convincing manner. "You'll be back on the ship for your morning tea."

"Gentlemen!" a harried-sounding Mr. O'Grady shouted. "Please step back. Allow the women and children to get on the boats. Mrs. Sanders, come this way please. You're going in this boat. I need you to take care of Master Mark Barclay."

"Yes, Mr. O'Grady," a woman responded.

Some people climbed into the lifeboat with us. I dared not look to see who they were.

"Mr. O'Grady," a man said, "my wife and daughter are ready to go."

"We're not loading third-class passengers yet," Mr. O'Grady pointed out. "You must take your family back to your room, Mr. Reed."

"My daughter is going on this boat," Mr. Reed insisted.

"I don't want to!" a little girl cried.

"Mr. Reed!" Mr. O'Grady yelled.

"Get in the boat, Cathy," Mr. Reed ordered. "Now!"

"That's enough!" shouted Mr. O'Grady.

"My wife must go with Cathy," Mr. Reed barked.

"Mrs. Reed will go on a different boat."

"But this one is half empty," Mr. Reed protested. "It can hold a lot more."

"I'm not sure about that," responded Mr. O'Grady. "The boats haven't been tested."

"What!" Mrs. Sanders exclaimed. "Get me out of here!"

"I want Mum," Cathy cried.

"No." Mr. O'Grady's voice was firm.

Fear grabbed my heart, and I envisioned our overloaded boat plunging into the ocean. Yikes! I couldn't swim! Mark was going to give me a lesson today, but...oh, nothing mattered anymore. I tried to throw Mark's legs off my body, but he held his legs firmly over my back. I couldn't move.

"Mrs. Sanders, the boat is safe," Mark said.

I thought he was saying that for my benefit as well. After all, what choice did I have? If I revealed myself, they wouldn't let me back on the *Titanic* because I wasn't wanted there. And they probably wouldn't let me stay in the lifeboat. So, any way you looked at my options, I would end up in the ocean. I held my breath and prepared for the lifeboat to smash into the water.

A dog howled. Other dogs barked.

"No Italians!" an Englishman shouted. "Go back to your cabins!"

Sounds of protest filled the air, but the Englishman continued to shout, "Italians, go back to your cabins now!"

"They're filled with water!" someone yelled.

"Then go to the dining room," the Englishman ordered.

A woman sobbed as men shouted opposing orders.

"Lower away with what you got."

"Pull up!"

"No, pull the other way!"

Our boat rocked up and down. They were having great difficulty lowering it. A man cursed. The boat dropped several feet. It shook and swung back and forth.

One man snapped, "We should have done the emergency drill this morning."

It took several minutes and many conflicting orders before the lifeboat started to move again. First up a few inches, then it was slowly lowered and suddenly it dropped into the ocean. Thud! The boat shook violently when it hit the water.

Oh, no! I thought as the boat began to move with the waves. *I'm going to be seasick again.*

Hmmmm. Hmmmm. Hmmmm. I tried to hold the food in my stomach, but it wouldn't stay down.

I felt Mark's legs relax. I tossed them off my back, threw the blankets aside, sat up quickly and put my head over the side of the boat.

"Ar-r-r-rggg!"

"Are you ill again?" Mark asked, rubbing my back.

"What's he doing here?" a pasty-looking matron demanded to know.

"Mrs. Sanders," Mark said, "Leroy is my best friend." He gave me a protective hug.

"He shouldn't be here. He's, he's…"

"Let the child be," an older lady ordered.

Mrs. Sanders snapped, "I'm not staying in this boat with a Negro, Mrs. Browning!"

"Then get out!" Mrs. Browning's eyes narrowed.

The women began to argue, and the other thirty people in the boat joined in. They all took sides.

A woman, who was wearing only a nightgown, said, "We don't want any more Negroes in America." She looked at me pointedly.

I felt a sinking feeling in my heart. What was I going to do?

"Lower away!" shouted a man from the top of the ocean liner.

I looked up to see another lifeboat coming down.

A man threw a woman from the upper deck into the lifeboat, seven feet below. The vessel was lowered another fifty feet to the water.

Maybe they would let me in that lifeboat, I thought. As the vessel moved closer to our boat, I heard raised voices. Oh, no! They were arguing in that boat, too.

"How did he get in my boat?" a lady with a nasal voice demanded to know. She was speaking to a ship's officer, but was pointing to a Chinese man who looked very scared. "Why did you leave my husband, and let him on?"

My shoulders dropped. If they did not want the Chinese man, I guessed I would not be welcomed in that vessel either.

Maybe I should jump out of the boat, I thought. My lifejacket would keep me afloat. I looked in the water. It was very dark. Pieces of ice were floating on the surface. I put my fingers in the ocean and pulled them out quickly. It was awfully cold. I knew I wouldn't live too long in the freezing water.

Screams from the ocean liner pierced the crisp air. The arguing stopped in the lifeboats, and everyone looked at the *Titanic*.

It was the first time I realized how huge the ship was. It was gargantuan! We were sixty feet away and I could not see the ship from one end to the other end.

As we rowed farther away, the ship's stern rose in the air.

"Come back," an Englishman on the ship shouted over a megaphone. "Come back and fill up the boats. You can load people from the lower deck."

"Row harder," a crewman in our boat yelled. "We must move away from the ship."

"But they want us to go back," Mark protested.

"No," the man said. "It's too late. We can't save them. The lower decks are under water."

The *Titanic* continued to tip toward the bow, and some passengers fell off the ship. Many were not wearing lifejackets. Ear-piercing sounds of panic came from the distressed vessel. A man jumped in the water. He was followed by another...and another...and another...

"Why are they doing that?" I asked. "Don't they realize they'll die?"

"What's happening?" someone in our lifeboat cried.

No one responded, because we all knew the answer. The impossible was happening. The *Titanic* was sinking.

A Jewish woman wearing a Star of David necklace was holding the oil lantern that provided the only light on our vessel. The light revealed the thin line of tears running down her right cheek. "Why don't they get in a boat?" she asked.

"There aren't enough lifeboats," the Irishman pulling an oar explained.

"What are you saying?"

"We thought the *Titanic* was unsinkable, so provisions were only made for twenty lifeboats."

"Oh dear, oh heavens," cried Mrs. Hillock. "My husband is still on board!"

"Let's go back and save him," a young woman urged.

"We can't," responded a nervous Scotsman who, despite the cold air, had beads of sweat on his forehead. "We have to get as far away from the ship as possible. If not, when it sinks, we're going to be sucked down with it."

We all watched helplessly as some of the ship's lights flickered and then went out.

When the lights came back on, music started playing.

I felt hopeful. I figured musicians wouldn't be playing if things hadn't improved. The problem was fixed. Dr. Wells was right. The best engineers built the *Titanic*. It was indestructible.

A loud crash shattered the myth. My mouth opened wide in awe as the ship broke in two. Gigantic, bright sparks, long funnels of steam, and chunks of coal blasted into the clear sky. Smoke and ash rained down on our boat.

The four people manning the oars started rowing harder. They were not quick enough for one lady who urged them to "move faster!" She picked dust particles off her clothes and cried, "My beautiful white dress is ruined!" Her eyes caught mine. "Do you know how much I paid for this?"

I hadn't a clue and I didn't care, especially at that instant. The dark mass that was the front of the ocean liner had completely disappeared beneath the water.

"This can't be happening!" someone yelled.

No, it wasn't, I tried to tell myself. I was dreaming again. Mark would soon wake me up from this nightmare.

Mark gripped my shoulder, but he did not tell me to wake up. I looked at his face and knew it was not a dream. Tears were rolling down Mark's face, and he began to muddle words. If Mr. Wardles were here, he'd say boys aren't supposed to cry. "Don't you want to grow up to be a man?" he'd ask. "Then stop blubbering and speak the King's English."

Except, I was not Mr. Wardles. I was Mark's best friend. So I put my arm around his shoulder and held him tight. But I didn't know what to say.

No one offered a suggestion.

"I want Mum and Dad," a little girl yelled. She looked to be about seven or eight years old. Her long, black hair was pulled to the back and tied with a big, red bow. "Mum," she cried again.

"Cathy," Mrs. Browning said in a soothing voice, "your parents are on an other boat. You'll see them soon."

Panicked cries for help mixed with the squeals of drowning rats and the howls of dogs.

The noises alarmed me.

Mark covered his ears and buried his face in my lap. All I could do was hug him.

I watched in horror as the stern suddenly rose above the Atlantic Ocean and stood up straight in the air! The big rudder was completely out of the water, yet the stern continued to float. It looked like one of the tall buildings in London that was built along the River Thames. Those buildings would be by the water forever. But how long would the rear section of the *Titanic* remain above the ocean?

The clanking and smashing sounds indicated that it wouldn't be long. I realized that everything, including the crew, passengers, and animals were being thrown into the ocean.

One funnel disappeared under the water. A huge explosion burst out of the second funnel before it, too, slipped under the surface.

The stern swayed slightly. Then like an injured whale, this castle of steel groaned and cried out in pain as it plunged into the ocean.

The *Titanic* was gone.

The howls of people drowning terrified me. I clung to Mark, stunned by how helpless we were. There was nothing we could do.

Some of the women in our boat began weeping. One woman clutched her big, shaggy dog and wailed, "What's going to happen to us?"

ADRIFT

People in the water yelled for help as they struggled to keep their heads above the surface. They screamed and screamed. Yet our lifeboat didn't move to rescue them.

"Do something!" Mark cried.

"We can't," a gray-haired lady responded. Her expression was as stiff as the cuffs on her coat sleeves.

"They'll all try to come on board." Mrs. Sanders' voice trembled. "That will sink our boat."

"But we could help a few," Mark insisted.

"We must save ourselves." Mrs. Sanders' mouth tightened.

I shuddered. How could we ignore the struggle of those people in the water? They needed us. They wanted to live. Yet no one did anything to help.

The screams continued. We listened to them for an hour. Then we heard nothing. We looked at each other. We looked in the water.

There was silence. Dead silence. And the lingering memory of the wretched, earsplitting screams.

This was scary.

What happened to everyone in the water? I looked at the people in our lifeboat. Their faces were as-white-as potatoes.

No one talked about throwing me out of the boat anymore. They were more worried about being rescued.

Mark started to cry again. He curled up on the bottom of the boat and hid his face in his hands.

I crouched in the bow and tried to control my seasickness. "The waters are calm," I told myself. "There are only small ripples in the ocean. I can handle this. It is possible to control motion sickness. It's mind over matter." Miss Owen used to say, "Use your mind to control the unruly impulses of your body."

It was working. I didn't feel sick anymore. I was just tired and cold.

An officer offered his overcoat to the woman who was wearing only a nightgown.

Mrs. Hillock and a passenger who left his jacket on the ship were shivering.

I wondered if Mrs. Hillock would accept a blanket from me. I slowly moved toward her and placed a blanket around her shoulders.

She accepted it with a nod of her head, but didn't say anything.

I offered another blanket to the man without a jacket.

His mouth twitched into a hint of a smile. "Thank you, young fella," he said in an accent that was similar to the angry passenger who wanted the steward to throw me off the *Titanic.*

I returned the man's smile, and his smile broadened. His response made me feel better. It was the first time a man had ever smiled at me or thanked me for anything.

The other boats had moved away from our lifeboat. As someone flashed a green light across the water, we realized that we were in the middle of a drifting ice field. Mountains of ice towered up to one hundred feet above the surface.

An outraged woman in a white fur coat voiced the question I wanted to ask, "Why didn't the crew see the danger?"

No one answered.

Something knocked against the side of the boat. It was a diary. I took it out of the water. It must have been on the ship, I thought.

Other things started to float around our vessel. There were flowers, newspapers, a door, a tablecloth, a photograph, hairnets, folding deck chairs, lots of paper money, an apple...

I grabbed the apple and gave it to Cathy. She took it, but she didn't stop crying.

There was no food in the boat, so I continued to look for some in the water. I found asparagus, a piece of bread, lettuce, and grapes.

"Oh, no!" Mark yelled. "My shoes are wet. The lifeboat is leaking!"

Mrs. Browning found a hole in the bottom of the boat. She placed a finger in the hole to plug it. But ice-cold water continued to rise around Mark's feet.

A young woman found a pail in the bow and began bailing water out.

I wondered how long our vessel could remain afloat. If the lifeboat sprung more leaks, we could sink.

The people with oars started to row faster. Our vessel moved closer to a group of lifeboats that had gathered together.

The survivors in the other boats looked just as-scared-as the ones in our vessel. Some prayed aloud. Others appeared to be numb with disbelief.

A few, however, were insensitive to the terrible trouble we were in.

"My bed!" a lady with a big hat bellowed, "I've lost my feather bed!" A few people tried to shut her up, but she continued to wail about her customized feather bed.

Another woman guzzled brandy from a bottle and picked arguments with several people.

One person was trying to quiet a dog yapping at a lady's pet pig. A pig! I couldn't believe that someone took a pig on the *Titanic* and into a lifeboat!

The Irishman told Mrs. Browning to take her fingers out of the hole. Then he plugged the hole with his finger.

"Mum!" I heard Cathy cry.

Looking over my left shoulder, I saw the little girl crawl out of our boat and into another.

A tiny woman pulled Cathy into her trembling arms. "Thank God you're alive," she sobbed. "Thank God you're alive."

"Mum," Cathy said, "where's Dad?"

I didn't hear the answer, but I did see tears run down the mother's face as she kissed her daughter's cheek.

When the temperature dropped several degrees, we drew closer to one another for warmth. Then silence fell over us.

Soon, I was lost in my own thoughts about the night. It was beautiful, clear, and moonless. The ocean was very calm, and the breeze was gentle.

My eyes were drawn to the bright lights in the sky. I recognized many of the constellations. There was the Big Dipper, Ursa Minor, Draco, Hercules, Corona Bor...

The heavenly sky appeared to be glowing. I thought it was the first light of Monday. As the minutes dragged by and the sun didn't rise, I realized that it must be the Northern Lights. I had read about them in Mark's astronomy book, but I had never seen them before.

I watched the columns of colors dance across the beautiful night sky.

"It's so wonderful to be alive!" Mrs. Browning exclaimed. "Isn't that a magnificent display of nature's artwork?"

I nodded.

Looking toward the east, I saw a constellation that I did not recognize. It was moving closer to us. I wondered if they were shooting stars.

I wanted to ask Mark what their names were, but his head was buried in his hands, and he was making little sobbing sounds.

The unfamiliar stars came closer and closer and got brighter and brighter. I had never seen stars like these before. "It's a ship!" I shouted excitedly.

"We're saved!" a woman exclaimed.

We all began shouting to attract the crew on the ship.

"Over here! Over here!" I screamed.

"It's coming!" a woman shouted.

The ship sounded its foghorn.

"That's the most wonderful sound I've ever heard!" someone blurted out.

I agreed.

The drunken woman stood up in her boat and waved at the ship.

"Sit down," a man ordered. "You'll capsize the boat."

When the woman refused to listen, the red-haired lady beside her became furious. In a surprising move, the redhead grabbed the drunken woman and pulled her down. Thud! The drunk fell hard on her bottom, and her feet flew in the air.

I had to laugh out loud. Mrs. Browning laughed too. Mrs. Sanders managed to part her lips in a weak attempt to smile.

The ship steamed toward us very slowly. It avoided hitting the icebergs that were still drifting in the ocean.

Some women were impatient for the ship to reach us, but I was willing to wait a little longer. I did not want our rescuers to sink, too.

An Englishman suggested that we row our boats toward the ship. We all agreed immediately. It was a relief to be heading somewhere instead of drifting aimlessly in the ocean.

As we moved forward, the Englishman shouted, "Now boys, sing!"

He led us in the song, "Row for the shore, boys." Our response was a feeble mixture of screeching voices. Within minutes, the Englishman put an end to our tuneless noise by suggesting that we cheer instead.

An hour passed. The water gradually began to swell. A powerful wave hit the side of our lifeboat. A French girl clutched a doll to her chest and cried out when our vessel sank lower in the water.

"Pull together," a crewman yelled at the women who were rowing.

A big wave crested in front of the bow.

We screamed. We prayed. We held on to one another as the wave came crashing into our boat. The freezing water drenched our clothes, but our boat remained afloat.

The woman with the pail fell to her knees in defeat. I grabbed the pail from her blistered hand and continued to bail the water out.

I was glad to be doing something. It made me feel as if I had control over the alarming situation. Soon, the water that was five inches high at the bottom of our boat became four inches, three, then two.

I relaxed my arms.

"Another big one!" a man shouted.

The boat rolled. I fell to the bottom, and water rushed into my mouth.

Someone grabbed my coat by the collar and yanked me up to a sitting position. I gulped, stammered, and tried to breathe normally again.

"Are you okay?"

I turned to face my rescuer. It was the man to whom I had given a blanket. "Yes, tha...than...thank you." The words sputtered out of my mouth.

He took the pail from my hand and bailed the water out.

The steamer stopped moving toward us. From its deck, a light shone onto the water's surface. Soon, I saw people moving from a lifeboat up the side of the ship.

There were so many survivors. The rescue dragged on for hours.

As dawn started to break, Mrs. Browning's eyes filled with tears. "I thought I'd never see another morning again," she said. "Isn't it the most beautiful sunrise?"

I agreed.

Finally, it was our turn to go on board the rescue ship, which had the name *Carpathia* painted on the side of the hull.

Mrs. Sanders and Mrs. Hillock insisted on being the first to be lifted onto the ship.

Mark's wet, cold feet were hurting him. He had to be placed in a canvas basket. It was attached to a rope that was thrown down from a deck forty feet above.

"Give me your bag," Mark said.

I handed it to him. Then I tightened the knot on the rope before yelling to the people above, "He's ready!"

Mark was lifted up to the railing of the top deck. Two men grabbed his basket and pulled him to safety.

The next basket was given to a woman and her shaggy dog.

I was told to climb a rope ladder that was thrown over the side of the *Carpathia*, but I was reluctant to climb it because my arms and legs were weak.

"Leroy," an impatient Scotsman shouted, "if you don't start climbing, you'll die here."

I took a deep breath and reached for the ladder. I put one hand above the other and pulled myself up.

The ladder swung toward the ship. My cap fell into the ocean. My knees smashed against the hull.

The rope ladder wrapped around my body when it swung away from the ship. A glove slipped off, and my left hand lost its grip on the rung.

When I tried to catch the glove, my left wrist scraped against the rope. The skin ripped. Blood spurted out. I screamed.

"What are you yelling about?" the Scotsman hollered. "Climb, lad! Climb!"

"I can't," I cried.

"Then get off the ladder and let me on."

"No!"

"You better get moving, because I have no intention of dying here!"

It took a few minutes for me to reposition my body on the ladder. Ignoring the blood running down my left hand, I placed it on the rung above my right hand and pulled myself up.

Halfway to the top, I heard screams from below. I was so startled, my shoes slipped off the rope. But I held on and soon regained my footing.

I looked down to see that an inflatable lifeboat had flipped over. People were in the ocean. Some were not wearing lifejackets. Three went under the water and didn't resurface. Then another person disappeared...and another...and another...

The Scotsman from my lifeboat was trying to save the drowning people, but the Atlantic Ocean took them all before he could rescue anyone.

There were cries from people on the ship, and cries from those below in lifeboats. I wanted to cry too. But I couldn't allow anything to unnerve me. It might cause me to lose my grip and I, too, would land in the ocean.

I rested my head against the ladder, closed my eyes, and breathed deeply to calm my fears.

"Are you all right, lad?" the Scotsman shouted from below.

"Yes," I answered.

"If you…"

"I'll make it," I said, cutting his words short. Then I put one hand above the other and continued my climb.

THE CARPATHIA

"Six hundred and seventy-nine," a sailor said when I dragged myself on board at 7:25 am.

"What?" I asked.

"You're the six hundred and seventy-ninth survivor."

"That's all?" My mouth opened wide in disbelief.

"Yes, yes," he responded sadly. His eyes moved to a young woman who clutched a baby to her chest as two men lifted her out of a basket. "Six hundred and eighty. Six hundred and eighty-one."

I looked over the railing. There was only one lifeboat left with survivors. There had to be others, I told myself. The *Titanic's* newspaper had said that the ship was carrying more than two thousand people. Where were they now? I looked across the water. Nothing. I saw absolutely nothing but the wide ocean, a whale, and icebergs stretching up into the clear blue sky. My shoulders dropped in despair.

Then a thought flashed into my mind. There must be survivors on the other side of the *Carpathia*. I wanted to see if that was the case, but I couldn't get across the overcrowded deck.

A gentle-looking Indian woman approached me and examined my injured hand. Her medicine stung as she cleaned and disinfected my wound, but I was too numb to cry.

Mrs. Browning handed me a sandwich.

"Thanks," I muttered.

Then someone gave me a beverage. It was coffee. Normally, I didn't like the smell of coffee, but at that moment, I welcomed the warmth of the drink as it went down my throat and settled my stomach.

"Leroy!"

I thought I heard someone yell my name. I stood up on a bench and peered over hundreds of heads.

"Leroy, I'm here!"

I spotted Mark on the other side of the deck. "I see you!" I yelled and waved wildly.

"He's taking me to a stateroom!" Mark shouted as a tall crewman carried him through a door.

"I'll find you!" I promised.

A broad hand fell on my left shoulder. I tried to wriggle out of the strong grasp, but the hand forced me to step down from the bench. Turning around, I looked into the hollow, green eyes of the steward who had chased me into *Titanic's* first-class lounge. My scream died in my throat.

"Come with me," he ordered. His right hand was bandaged, so he used his left hand to push me forward.

I wanted to protest, but I couldn't find my voice. Even if I had one, who was going to help me? Mark was gone, and Mrs. Browning was nowhere in sight.

I thought the steward was going to throw me overboard, but we were moving down a narrow stairway.

"Where are we going?" I finally had the nerve to ask.

"To steerage," he answered.

"What's there?"

"Third-class passengers and crew."

I was shocked. "You're not going to toss me in the ocean?" My voice shook with fear.

"Enough people have already died today, don't you think so?"

"Yes," I agreed. "More than enough."

"I'm glad to see that you survived," he said in a sincere tone of voice.

I was tempted to ask him why he was glad, but I feared I would get an answer I wouldn't want to hear.

"Do you want to remain alive?" The steward's words sent a chill across my back.

"Yes," I murmured, wishing I could make my voice sound stronger.

The steward opened a cabin door and shoved me onto a bunk bed. "Stay away from the first-class section," he ordered. "This is where you will sleep. Have a good rest." As suddenly as he appeared, he vanished, closing the door behind him.

I slept the whole day. I woke up in the evening only to eat. Then I went back to sleep again.

Tuesday, I asked about Mark. I was shown a list of names of survivors and the location on the ship where they were sleeping.

Despite the steward's warning, I wanted to visit my best friend. The only way I could do this was to change my appearance. So I sorted through the mound of clothes that the *Carpathia*'s passengers donated to the survivors, and I created a disguise.

I found gloves and a floorlength overcoat. Turning up the coat collar so that the tip of the collar touched my nose, I eagerly approached a mirror. I viewed my reflection with a sense of satisfaction. This would work, I thought. Once I found the right hat, no one would realize I was a Negro.

The perfect hat was buried under a pile of socks. I tapped the sides of the hat back into shape and put it on. The rim slipped over my forehead and rested on my nose.

Since I could not see straight ahead, I kept my eyes on the floor as I made my way to the first-class section.

"Good morning," I said when I approached two pairs of shoes that were moving toward me. But I hurried down the hallway before anyone responded.

Seeing no more shoes ahead, I used my gloved right hand to slowly raise the hat off my nose and lift it above my eyes. No one was in sight.

I moved quickly from door to door in search of Mark's room. I found his room number and was thrilled when his familiar voice responded to my knock.

"Leroy!" Mark's face lit up when I opened the door. "No one knew where you were. I was so worried."

"I'm all right," I assured him as I removed my jacket.

"Why are you dressed like that?"

"I needed a disguise to get into the first-class section."

"They're prejudiced on this ship too!"

I smiled. "At least they aren't trying to throw me off." I sat on the bed. "How are you?"

"My feet are frostbitten. The doctor said if I rubbed them, they'd feel better in a couple of days."

"That's good, Mark."

"I can't wait to get to America."

I groaned before I could stop myself.

"What's wrong?" he asked.

"I won't be able to get into the country."

"Why?"

"A crewman said that when ships arrive in New York City, passengers are sent to Ellis Island. There, government officials decide who will be allowed into America."

"That doesn't apply to first-class passengers," Mark noted. "My steward said that as soon as the ship docks, my aunt can take me home."

"I'm not a first-class passenger, and I'm a Negro. Remember, the woman in the lifeboat told us that they don't want any more Negroes in America."

Mark pointed to my hat. "If you wear that disguise, no one will recognize that you're a Negro. You can walk with me among the first-class passengers."

He had a good idea, I thought. "It's worth a try," I said. "Everyone will be so glad to be in New York, maybe no one will pay attention to me."

"Exactly." His eyes looked at me intently. "So you will do it, Leroy?"

I hesitated before answering, "Yes. I pray this works. The thought of being sent back to England..."

Mark didn't give me a chance to complete my sentence. "I won't let that happen to my best friend," he said.

"How long will our friendship last?"

He looked shocked. "What kind of question is that?"

"Will you be my friend in America?" I surprised Mark and myself by what my question implied.

"Of course," he responded hastily. "Our friendship is indestructible."

"That's what was said about the *Titanic*."

"I don't want to talk about that ship again." His lips were drawn in a thin line. "As for our friendship..."

"I don't see how we can continue it," I said. "To be with you, I have to hide, sneak around, wear disguises, and..."

"Leroy, I'm your friend. I can't do very much about how adults treat you now. When I grow up, I hope to change things. But, in the meantime, I don't want to lose your friendship."

I decided to believe Mark. The alternative was too painful to consider. I exaggerated a yawn in an attempt to change the subject. "A crying baby kept me up most of the night," I lied.

"You can nap here."

"No," I responded hastily, fearing that his host, an American businessman, might be angry if he returned and found me resting in his stateroom. "I'd rather sleep in my room."

"Take this," Mark said as I rose to my feet. He handed me my bag with the treasure box still inside. "Thanks for coming."

"I'll be back tomorrow," I promised, pulling my hat down on my face before I left the room.

The next morning, the hallway leading to Mark's stateroom was very crowded, so I returned to third class. As I walked down the stairs, I saw a girl sitting on the bottom step.

"Cathy," I said, "are you all right?"

She raised her pale, tear-stained face, but didn't appear to recognize me. "Have you seen my father?" she asked.

"No," I answered. I was going to tell her that I had no idea what her father looked like, but I knew that wasn't the answer she wanted to hear. So I said, "The crew has the list of survivors. They'll tell you where to find him."

Cathy choked back a sob. "I've seen the list. Dad isn't on it."

Oh, no! That meant that her father was probably dead. I stared at her scruffy, black patent leather shoes as I searched my brain for words of comfort. "I'm sorry," was all I was finally able to say.

Cathy burst into tears. I reached for her hand. It was as-cold-as the iceberg. Not knowing what else to do, I sat on the stairs with her.

I left Cathy in the middle of the afternoon and went to visit Mark. I read aloud to him, while he rubbed his feet. After a couple of hours, he took his first steps around the stateroom.

Mark grinned. "Tomorrow, I'll see daylight."

"Are you positive that you're strong enough to walk about the ship?"

"Yes." His voice was very firm. "I need to get out of this room. It doesn't even have a porthole."

"The weather is very bad," I told him. "There isn't much to see."

This news did not discourage Mark. He insisted that he would meet me on the upper deck the next morning.

Thick fog enveloped the Carpathia as it continued to make its way across the Atlantic on Thursday. As I walked on the upper deck in the morning, it was difficult to see people who were a few feet away from me. I wandered around in the fog for an hour before I found Mark. He was sitting under the British flag that was flying at half-mast in memory of the 1500 people who were lost.

As the sun rose higher in the sky, the fog slowly faded away. Soon, more survivors appeared on deck. They were still mourning. Some were crying. Many were praying aloud. Others sat by themselves and gave the impression that they wanted to be left alone.

A few survivors were involved in heated arguments.

"I should never have traveled on a ship with Captain Smith," an old man grumbled. "Remember that accident he had on the *Olympic*?"

A young man protested. "Mr. Dixon, the *Oceanic Steam Navigation Company* said it wasn't his fault."

"Well, I think it was!"

"What's the *Oceanic Steam Navigation Company*?" I ventured to ask.

The two men looked at me as if they were surprised I had joined their conversation. They stared at me for so long, I thought that they were not going to respond. So I turned to leave.

"The *Oceanic Steam Navigation Company* is the official name of the *White Star Line*." It was the young man who answered. "They're building another ship that will be bigger than the *Titanic*. I think it's called…" He scrunched his eyebrows in an effort to recall the name.

Mr. Dixon helped him out. "The *Gigantic*." He ran his bony right hand through his thinning, brown hair. "I hope they put enough lifeboats on that one."

Mrs. Browning joined the discussion. "They shouldn't call a ship 'unsinkable.' It tempts fate."

"The *Titanic* was going too fast," Mr. Dixon growled.

"All this hurry to reach New York," Mrs. Browning added. "Look where it got us."

Mark and I didn't want to hear any more arguing, so we walked over to Cathy. I was glad to see that she was brushing a dog's hair instead of crying. This time, she recognized me and greeted me with a little smile.

A group of children were sitting close by listening to a very old sailor tell tales. Cathy, Mark, and I decided to listen too.

The sailor's name was Daniel, but he said that the crew called him Graybeard because he had a fuzzy, gray beard. He was eighty-three years old. He was the oldest person I had ever met.

Although his days as an active crewman were long over, Graybeard said he stayed on the *Carpathia*, because the ship was the only home he had.

"When I was a youn' laddie," Graybeard said in a thick Irish accent, "my parents were so poor, had to leave home at eight to seek my fortune. 'Twas the time of the potato famine. There was no work on the farms, so I went to sea." He told us about his many adventures. He had been in three shipwrecks, had fought with pirates, and there had been one mutiny.

It sounded interesting, but it wasn't the life I wanted to lead. The sinking of the *Titanic* was more than enough excitement for ten lifetimes! All I wanted now was a place to call home.

At teatime, a tired-looking crewman brought us sandwiches and coffee.

"What will happen when we get to New York City?" Cathy asked.

We all looked to the crewman for an answer.

"You had a third-class ticket." The crewman's response was more of a statement than a question.

"Yes," Cathy answered.

"Well, it depends," he said.

"On what?" she asked.

The crewman handed her a sandwich before answering. "People are waiting at the city dock to see if their family members survived. If someone is there for you, the government will make an exception and allow you in."

"Mum and I know no one in America," Cathy cried.

"Then you must go to Ellis Island."

AMERICA

Boom! Crash!! Crack!!! Thunder and lightning controlled the night sky.

Dressed in our overcoats and hats, Mark and I stayed on the top deck of the *Carpathia* to watch the magical, raging storm.

Suddenly, there were a thousand lights in the distance. "Look at that!" I shouted. "I've never seen so many before."

"That's New York City," Mark said.

"Wow!" was all I could say.

"Lady Liberty is over there!" Graybeard pointed out.

The frame of the famous statue towered above New York Harbor. I couldn't see the details, but a picture of the statue, which I had seen in a book, was etched into my mind.

"It's so big," an Irishwoman remarked with a mixture of joy and awe.

People around us were suddenly changed from grieving survivors to immigrants ready to embrace the statue's promise of freedom and opportunity.

The mood soured when newspapermen in little boats approached the ship. The rough waves could have destroyed the boats, yet the newsmen continued to pursue their story. They used megaphones to bark their demands for information about the tragedy.

The survivors did not respond.

The *Carpathia* crawled toward the city.

Graybeard said, "We passed the Cunard pier." A puzzled expression was on his face. "Where are we going?"

He soon had his answer. The *Carpathia* stopped at the *White Star* pier and dropped off the fourteen lifeboats. Then it docked at the Cunard pier around 9:00 p.m. Newsmen tried to come on board, but the crew wouldn't allow it.

The rain changed to light drizzle as passengers prepared to leave the *Carpathia*. Survivors in first class were the first to walk down the gangway.

"Order!" a man shouted. "Do not rush the pier."

I turned up my coat collar, straightened my gloves, picked up my bag, pulled my hat down to my nose, took a deep breath, and held on to Mark's arm.

People bounced against me. They talked over my head. Someone stepped on my toes. An elbow almost knocked my hat off my head. But no one stopped us as Mark led me through the crowd of first-class passengers and past the government agents.

"We did it!" Mark said, moving my hat up to my forehead.

I raised my hands in triumph as I looked around me. "I am really in America."

Mark jumped up and down, and I laughed and danced in a puddle of rainwater.

"What happened on the *Titanic*?" A newspaperman almost knocked me to the ground in his haste to question the gentleman in front of me.

"Did your husband die?" a rude newsman asked a lady.

The pushy reporters swarmed around the survivors, hounding them for stories.

Many survivors refused to talk about the tragedy. Others were very eager to tell their version of the disaster.

Thankfully, no one asked Mark or me for our version. I was a little surprised. I guessed the stories of children on the *Titanic* were not as-big-as the adults' stories. So, we avoided the newsmen and started searching for Mark's aunt.

"What does she look like?" I asked, looking at the hundreds of people around us. Some were hugging each other. A few were crying. Others seemed lost and confused.

Mark and I walked around the pier looking for his aunt whom he described as a tall, blonde lady with blue eyes. An hour passed. Most of the first-class passengers were gone. Second-class passengers were given permission to leave the *Carpathia*. They were now searching the crowds for relatives and friends. Confusion surrounded us.

The people from the Salvation Army were everywhere. They wore black hats and dark, military-style overcoats. Some of the men helped the injured into vehicles, while the women offered food, clothing, and shelter to able-bodied survivors.

"Are you going to Pennsylvania?" a man wearing a railroad cap asked survivors as they stepped off the gangway, "We have free train tickets for you."

"I'm going to Indiana," an Englishwoman said.

"We can give you a free ride to Pennsylvania, but you have to pay for the rest of your journey."

"I'll take it," she said.

"Go to that taxi." The man nudged the woman toward a vehi-cle that already had one passenger in the back seat. "It will take you to the Pennsylvania Railroad."

Some survivors received offers of help from the staffs of Brook-lyn Hospital, Lebanon Hospital, St. Vincent Hospital, and the Shel-tering Society.

We received offers, too. Mark rejected them and reassured me that his aunt would be there soon. But she was nowhere in sight. We wandered around the pier for another half-hour. Finally, a lady from the Salvation Army insisted that we accept her offer of a hot cup of tea. I drank mine gratefully.

"There she is!" Mark waved his hands frantically. He was trying to attract the attention of a striking blonde lady who was carry-ing a white umbrella. She was standing next to a street lamp. "Aunt Helen, here I am!"

Mark's aunt ran up and hugged him. She squeezed him so tightly, Mark looked as though he were being squashed. "Thank God you're okay!" she said over and over between kisses. "I'm so sorry that I wasn't here when you arrived. The newspaper said that the *Carpathia* wouldn't dock until midnight."

Her accent made me nervous. It was similar to the accent of the angry passenger who wanted to throw me off the *Titanic*. Would she…?

I refused to complete the thought, but I did look around for the people from the Salvation Army. I thought that I might have to accept their offer of a warm place where I could spend the night.

A large group from the Salvation Army was at the foot of the *Carpathia*'s gangway. They were greeting third-class passengers who were finally being allowed off the ship. I drew a sharp breath when I saw Cathy and her mother standing in line at the top of the gangway. Were they on their way to Ellis Island?

I would have been in that line. But mercifully, Mark had saved me from that fate. I looked up to the gray sky and expressed a silent thank-you.

"Aunt Helen," Mark said, "this is my best friend, Leroy. Leroy, this is my aunt, Miss Barclay."

"Hello, Leroy." The warmth in her voice erased any fears I had about her disliking me. "It's nice to meet you," she said.

"It's nice to meet you, too, Miss Barclay."

"I brought Leroy with me," Mark continued. "He's an orphan. So, he needs to be adopted, too."

"Oh!" Her face brightened. "I know the perfect parents for you."

"You do?" I asked, amazed.

She nodded her head slightly. "A wonderful couple. They've always wanted a child! They don't have any of their own."

"When can I meet them?"

"Very soon, Leroy." She reassured me with her friendly smile.

It started to rain again as she ushered us across the street. We passed several ambulances and a couple who was getting wet as they sat in an open car.

Mark's aunt led us to a vehicle that smelled brand new.

"A closed car!" The words blurted out of my mouth.

She responded with a knowing wink. "This is a Cadillac. It's one of the first cars ever built that is completely enclosed. I hated driving in open cars. Whenever I did, my clothes were ruined."

Her car was extraordinarily fancy with several options. There was a clock, a windshield, and an electric horn.

"You drive!?" I exclaimed as Miss Barclay started the electric ignition.

"I believe a woman can do anything a man can do," she stated. "I learned to drive after my father died last year. He didn't believe men and women were equal. If he found out I thought this way, he would have disowned me like he disowned Mark's father."

"You drive very well," I said honestly.

"Thank-you." She seemed genuinely pleased with my compliment. "Leroy, was your mother French?"

"I never knew my mother, Miss Barclay. Why do you ask?"

"Because Leroy is a French name. It means 'the king.'"

"Really?" My huge, brown eyes revealed my surprise.

"Yes," Miss Barclay said. "Your mother must have thought you were very special to have given you such a significant name."

"He is special," Mark said.

"He would have to be if he is your friend," Miss Barclay said.

As they continued to speak about me in glowing terms, I relaxed. It was so wonderful to be in the company of people who liked me. I may not have been the king, but these friendly people were treating me very well. And I loved it.

"Where are we going?" I asked.

"To my apartment. It's on the Upper East Side of Manhattan," she answered.

"Manhattan?"

"It's one of the boroughs that make up New York City. There are four other boroughs—the Bronx, Brooklyn, Queens, and Staten Island. They're large districts within the city." She turned a corner. "We're on Fifth Avenue," she stated.

"I read about this street in a book," I told her. "It has a lot of fancy houses and stores."

She nodded. "It's where I shop." She drove slowly, because the rain had once again turned into a thunderstorm. I looked out the car window, but I couldn't see a thing.

"This isn't a good night to be sightseeing," she noted. "We'll leave that for another day."

That was fine with me. I was exhausted and just wanted a warm place to rest my head.

The car stopped in front of a ten-story apartment building. "That's Central Park," she said, pointing across the street. "Tomorrow, you can play there."

Mark's aunt lived on the top floor. Her spacious home was furnished like the *Titanic*, but I was too disillusioned by my experience on that ship to get excited by wealth anymore.

"Is anybody hungry?" she asked as we followed her into the kitchen.

"Yes," Mark and I answered in unison, taking seats at a small table.

"My housekeeper has the night off," Miss Barclay explained as she opened a cupboard. "Tonight, the best thing I can offer you is cookies and strawberry jam sandwiches."

"I love strawberry jam," Mark responded enthusiastically.

My eyes fell on a paper that was placed at a corner of the table. It was the telegram Mark sent from the *Titanic*. It read:

Aunt Helen, I was afraid to go on Titanic.
My friend, Leroy, said it'd be O.K.
It's better than O.K. Thanks for great
room. Love, Mark.

A tear rolled down my cheek. I quickly wiped it away. I hadn't cried when the *Titanic* sank. If I started now, I probably would never stop. It wouldn't be good for Miss Barclay to see me as a crybaby. She'd never find anyone to adopt someone like that. I just had to hold back my tears and cry later in bed.

Mark devoured his aunt's sandwiches and the milk, while I tried to swallow a cookie and the lump in my throat.

Miss Barclay sat at the table and started talking. Neither Mark nor I responded until she mentioned that a building in the city had a telescope.

Mark's face lit up. "Can I go there?" he asked.

"Yes." She seemed pleased to have found something that interested her nephew. "Leroy, do you want to go, too?"

I hesitated.

"Tired?" she asked when I failed to answer her question.

I nodded.

She allowed me to leave the table and go to bed.

The next afternoon, Mark and I explored Central Park. I was amazed that it was so big. We swam in a lake, climbed trees, played ball and many other games.

When we returned to the apartment, Miss Barclay introduced us to guests she had invited to dinner. "Leroy and Mark," she began, "This is Mr. and Mrs. Clark. Mr. Clark is a real estate agent, and Mrs. Clark and I co-edit a weekly newspaper."

My face brightened. They were Negroes like me. Mr. Clark was tall and muscular. He was dressed in a handsomely-tailored, dark suit.

Mrs. Clark was a short lady with thick, black hair. She was wearing a simple, silk hat. Her dress was green, and she had a lace shawl around her shoulders.

"Good evening," Mark and I responded.

Mr. Clark greeted Mark, then stretched out his large right hand to me. He gave my hand a warm squeeze. "It's nice to meet you, young man."

"It's nice to meet you, too, Sir."

Mrs. Clark leaned toward me, spreading the rose scent of her perfume. "Welcome to New York," she said in a voice that sounded as if she were singing.

"Thank-you." I smiled. "You smell wonderful," I remarked.

She beamed in response. "My husband gave me the perfume for my birthday."

"You have good taste, Sir."

Now it was Mr. Clark's turn to beam. His words of thanks were accompanied with a look of affection for me. "Leroy, how do you like our city?"

"It's beautiful." I grinned.

"The only thing he's seen is the park," Miss Barclay commented as she directed us into the dining room.

"There's so much to do there!" I exclaimed. "We rowed in a boat, fed the swans, played hide and seek and..." I suddenly stopped talking because I remembered that Mr. Wardles said that adults do not like children who never shut up. And I did want these adults to like me very much.

Mark pulled a chair away from the table so that his aunt could sit down.

Mr. Clark did the same for his wife. "I can show you some of the park's secrets," he offered.

"Will you?" I smiled.

"Is Saturday all right?"

"Yes!"

"Good. We'll spend the day in the park."

I was happy. I had never known a man who wanted to spend an entire day with a boy.

The steak dinner was great. So were the jokes and stories Mr. Clark told. He was the funniest man I had ever met. He made us all laugh, even Mark who hadn't smiled much since the disaster.

Mrs. Clark's laugh sounded like music. I guessed that must be why Mr. Clark married her.

After we ate our cake, the Clarks talked in private with Miss Barclay. Then Mrs. Clark asked me to sit beside her on the sofa in the living room. "I hear that you're looking for a new home, Leroy," she said.

I nodded my head.

"We'd like to give you that home."

I was speechless. I felt tears in my eyes. I tightened my throat, because I didn't want them to see me cry.

Mrs. Clark took my right hand. "We want to be your parents. Would you like to be our son?"

"Yes!"

"Wonderful!" Mr. Clark clapped me on the back. "On Monday, we'll go to the government office and make it official."

Mrs. Clark kissed and hugged me. She hugged me as tightly as Mark's aunt had hugged him.

At last someone wanted me.

Later that evening, I thanked Mark and his aunt. Then, I left with the Clarks. They took me to the north end of Central Park.

"We're in Harlem," Mr. Clark announced. "This is our house."

I was going to live in a house! It was a big, two-story townhouse.

Mrs. Clark put my coat on a hook in the foyer. "Your bedroom is upstairs."

I ran up the steps.

"Hey!' my new father shouted. "Wait for us." He ran behind me.

I dashed into the room on my right. "Is this it?" I asked.

"Yes," he said. "My wife made the bed for you."

Mrs. Clark entered the room. "You can decorate this place any way you want," she said.

I felt like singing for joy as I jumped on the bed. "Can I invite Mark over?"

"Yes," Mr. Clark said.

Mrs. Clark tucked me into bed. "What's this?" she asked, pointing to the bag I had placed on the nightstand.

"My treasure box," I replied, taking it out of the bag. "I have a gift inside for you."

"A gift for me!" She looked surprised.

I opened the box and took out a green scarf. "When I was a baby, someone left me at a bakery. This scarf was wrapped around me, and a piece of paper with my name was pinned to it. It's my favorite thing."

"It's so precious," she said. "You shouldn't give it away."

"I believe the scarf belonged to my mother, and that's all she had to give me. Since you're going to be my new mother, I'd like you to have it."

"Thank you, Leroy." She kissed me again. "I'll treasure it always."

Mr. Clark sat on the other side of my bed. "Would you like me to tell you a story?" he asked.

"Yes, please!"

He made a big production of clearing his throat. Then, with a devilish grin, he began. "It's about a mischievous spider named Anancy, and his arch enemy, a dragonfly."

His performance made his wife and me chuckle.

When he finished, I asked, "Can you tell us another story, Mr. Clark?"

"Not tonight, Leroy. Tomorrow you have to go to school."

"School? Wow! Maybe I will get the opportunity to be a lawyer."

"A lawyer." Mr. Clark echoed my words. "Honey," he said to his wife, "we have a smart son."

I grinned. "I had the highest marks in my class, Mr. Clark."

"If you want, you can call me *Dad*." His eyes almost begged.

"And you can call me *Mum*," Mrs. Clark added softly.

I smiled and tried the words in my mouth. "Mum. Dad." Finally I had a Mum and a Dad, and a home in America.

AUTHOR'S COMMENTS AND HISTORICAL NOTES

The *R.M.S. Titanic* has fascinated me for years, but I always wondered why there were no stories of blacks on the famous ocean liner. My initial research led me to the fact that after the tragedy, many people believed that blacks were not on the *Titanic*.

Wealthy white Americans owned stock in the *White Star Line*, a shipping company that had a contract to transport England's mail across the seas. The names of the company's ships began with "Royal Mail Steamer", which was abbreviated to R.M.S.

The most lucrative part of the company's business was the transportation of large numbers of people moving from Europe to North America. Most of the immigrants were poor whites who sought a better life in the West.

A few immigrants were black. Some of these blacks descended from slaves In the British Empire. Others were descendants of American blacks who had moved to Britain after fighting on the English side during the American Revolution and the War of 1812. After England abolished slavery in 1838, some blacks became members of the middle class, but the majority were poor.

There were approximately twenty thousand blacks in England at the beginning of the twentieth century. Many black men worked in the shipping industry, while a significant number of black women were house servants. There were fewer black women than men. So, interracial marriages and relationships were common, especially among the poor.

Poor people of all colors were victims of many tragedies. They often died early due to disease, homelessness, starvation, or injuries they suffered as a result of the dangers of their jobs. When the poor were unable to care for their young, their children were sometimes abandoned.

Many of these children were placed in orphanages. A few were eventually adopted. But cross-cultural adoptions rarely occurred in England, or America, until the end of the twentieth century.

Orphans in England had to work to earn their keep. By the mid-nineteenth century, the British government required that all children attend school for at least a half day. But many factory owners disobeyed the law. They forced children to work up to twelve hours per day. By the beginning of the twentieth century, if adults were supportive, children up to the age of twelve could get a full day of schooling.

Unlike the Americans, the English taught blacks how to read even during slavery. Male slaves also studied mathematics, science, and other subjects as part of their training to be sailors. Religious groups were active in the education process. They developed literacy programs that promoted their values through the reading of the Bible.

In the early 1900s, the British wanted to be dominant over the sea. They were in a race with Germany, who shared the same goal.

Both countries invested a lot of money in the crafts and technologies that supported shipbuilding. This resulted in the first arms race of the twentieth century, which saw the two countries building large advanced navies that would eventually battle each other in World War I.

Before that Great War started in 1914, shipping companies who were involved in trade had their own commercial competition. The *Cunard Line* and the *White Star Line* in England competed to see who could build the biggest, fastest, and most luxurious superliners to transport the many immigrants moving to North America.

In 1907, *Cunard Line* had two stars on the ocean—the *Lusitania* and the *Mauritania*. They were the fastest and grandest ocean liners at the time. That year, the *White Star Line* decided to build the first of three luxurious sister ships that would be more than fifty percent bigger than the *Lusitania*.

The *White Star Line* launched the *Olympic* on October 20, 1910, the *Titanic* on May 31, 1911, and the *Britannic* on February 26, 1914. The original name of the third sister ship was *Gigantic*. But after the *Titanic* tragedy, the company wanted to downplay the super size of the third ship. So the *White Star Line* gave the new superliner the patriotic sounding name of a decommissioned ship that had serviced the company well from 1874 to 1899.

The *White Star*'s superliners were not as-fast-as *Cunard*'s ships. But on her maiden voyage, the *White Star* tried to attract as much publicity as possible by pressing the *Titanic* to arrive in New York City ahead of schedule.

Despite the fierce competition between the shipping companies, it is interesting to note that *Cunard* owned the *Carpathia*, the ship that rescued the survivors of the *Titanic* disaster.

People of different colors lived in the same London neighborhoods during the 1800s and the early 1900s. This was due to the fact that unlike America where whites and blacks lived in segregated communities, the British were more concerned about separating people by class rather than by race.

This did not mean that blacks in England did not experience prejudice. As more people became unemployed in the early 1900s, whites took out their anger on blacks. The mass immigration to North America helped to decrease the tensions, which were caused by poverty that not only existed in Britain, but also in other European countries.

Not every immigrant found a home in the West. First and second-class passengers quickly passed through immigration, but immigrants in third class had to go through a detailed screening process.

In New York City, third-class passengers were sent by ferry to Ellis Island where they were screened for undesirable traits. In certain instances, this resulted in their being sent back to Europe.

If they were permitted to enter the country, many third-class passengers could not afford to travel elsewhere. So, the majority stayed in New York City where it was easy to find work. Many of the poor worked in factories. Children as young as twelve years old worked eighty-four hours a week in the factories. Some girls and women made blouses, which were called shirtwaists at the beginning of the 20th century. On March 25, 1911 a fire at the Triangle Shirtwaist Factory killed 146 people. Despite these dangers, immigrants continued to arrive in the big city.

Americans from other states also moved to New York City in search of jobs and opportunities to live better lives. American Negroes were not welcomed, yet they came.

In 1626, eleven Africans were the first slaves on Manhattan Island. They were the first of many blacks who helped to build the city. All the slaves in the state of New York were freed in 1827.

By the middle of the 1800s, blacks were only allowed to live in the Five Points section of Lower Manhattan. As more European immigrants moved to the city, Blacks were forced to move north to a slum that was given the name Little Africa. In 1903, the Little Africa neighborhood was destroyed to build the Pennsylvania Railroad Station. After 277 years with a black population in New York City, the *Gilded Age* began without blacks having had the opportunity to live in decent neighborhoods in America's most prosperous city.

It was not until 1904 that blacks were allowed to purchase or rent respectable houses in Harlem, located at the north end of Manhattan Island. This was the result of the enterprise of the college-educated, African-American, Philip A. Payton, Jr., owner of the Afro-American Realty Company.

White-owned businesses such as the newspaper, *Harlem Home News,* called this development—"the invasion of Negroes". The newspaper strongly opposed the movement of African-Americans to Harlem, which had previously been a rural community where wealthy whites built country homes where they spent their weekends and summers. The newspaper was unable to stop black Americans from migrating to New York City.

At the same time, liberal white women were reaching out to blacks. Some of these women were suffragettes who wanted African-Americans to join them in their fight to get the vote for all Americans regardless of gender or color. After the 1911 Triangle fire, some of these white women also sought the assistance of the black women in an effort to establish a union for the female garment workers. This union would force employers to provide a safe work environment, better pay, and better work conditions for females.

At the beginning of the twentieth century, America had successfully invaded several nations whose population had many people of color. This included Cuba, the Philippines and countries in South America. Although white politicians and businessmen viewed this achievement as an opportunity to expand American trade, they did not want people of color from these countries to move to America and participate in its politics or its growing economy. As a result, measures were introduced to limit or deny entry to America for people of color.

At the same time, new Jim-Crow laws were excluding African-Americans from many opportunities that they were given when slavery was completely abolished in America after the Civil War. In some states, blacks were not allowed to ride on some streetcars or steamboats. Many railroad companies established Jim-Crow laws that permitted blacks to travel only in second or third class. On certain trains, they were refused transportation.

Since the owners of American railroad companies had invested in the *Titanic*, it is not surprising that Americans came to believe that the Jim-Crow laws extended to the *Titanic*. And since the superliner was a special ship, many presumed that blacks were not allowed on this vessel that transported the cream of white society.

Although Booker T. Washington sent his condolences when the *Titanic* sank, many African-American newspapers did not report the tragedy, cover the U.S. Senate hearings, or print any survivor stories. These actions, or inactions, helped give rise to the belief that blacks were not on the ship.

This view was reinforced by rumors about Jack Johnson, the famous African-American heavyweight-boxing champion, who tried to sail on the *Titanic*. The White Star would not sell Johnson a first-class ticket. The boxer was offered a second-class cabin, but he decided to sail on a different ship that allowed him to sleep in a first class stateroom. Johnson's story was popularized in songs performed by black entertainers. The famous Leadbelly sung a version of the song that said—

Captain Smith hollered, "I ain't haulin' no coal."

The song then notes that blacks should be thankful because no blacks were lost on the *Titanic*.

However, at least one black met his doom on the ship. The blacks who survived the tragedy were very young, light-skinned children who did not speak English. This created a remarkable situation; it was several decades before Americans became aware that blacks traveled on the *Titanic*.

These black survivors spoke only French. Because they returned to France within a few days of their arrival in New York City, they were not counted among the many survivors who traveled across America and told their version of the disaster. It should be noted, at this point, that members of this family were very traumatized by the tragedy and did not tell their story to outsiders until 1985.

These survivors were of mixed race. Three-year-old Simone Anne Marie and two-year-old Louise were the interracial children of Juliette Marie Louise Laroche, a white French woman, and Joseph Laroche, a black Haitian engineer.

Racial prejudices in France hampered Joseph's career ambitions, so he decided to move his family to Haiti where he knew he could get a good-paying engineering job. His mother was so overjoyed that he was coming home, she bought tickets for the family on the French ship, *La France*. However, *La France* did not allow children to eat with their parents in the dining room. So, the family decided to sail on the *Titanic*. Their second-class tickets allowed them to eat with their children in the second-class dining room. Children were not allowed to eat in *Titanic's* first-class dining saloon.

On April 10, 1912, the Laroche family traveled from their Paris home to Cherbourg, France. The family had to take a ferry out to the *Titanic*, because the ocean liner was too big to dock.

Mr. and Mrs. Laroche slept with their two daughters in a second-class cabin. Mr. Laroche felt the ocean liner collide with the iceberg. When he realized that the ship was sinking, he woke his wife and children and brought them up to the deck. Joseph spoke both English and French, so he asked the English-speaking crew to put his pregnant wife and two daughters on a lifeboat. Joseph remained on the ship and went down with it.

Juliette clutched the children to her chest during the terrible hours in the lifeboat. At some point, water started rising in the vessel, and a lady had to put her finger in the hole to stop the leak. The freezing water caused Juliette's feet to suffer frostbite. She had to be lifted up to the *Carpathia* in a canvas bag.

Once they arrived in New York City, the family received medi-cal treatment at St. Vincent Hospital. They were also the recipi-ents of many acts of kindness, including offers of clothes and money.

Since her husband was dead, Madame Laroche had no idea how she would support herself in Haiti. So she decided to return to her childhood home. But Madame refused to step foot on a British ship again. Passage was booked for her and her children on the French ship, *S.S. Chicago*. They arrived in France twenty days after they left on the *Titanic*'s maiden voyage. They never traveled on another ship again.

A week before Christmas, Madame Laroche gave birth to her husband's only son. Six years later, she won $20,000 in a lawsuit she had filed against the *White Star Line*. The money was used to start a successful home-based business. In 1980 Madame Laroche died at the age of 91. The following words were placed on her gravestone:

Wife of Joseph Laroche lost at sea

on RMS TITANIC, April 15th 1912.

With regards to the racism on the *Titanic*, the *White Star Line* eventually apologized for the poor treatment of Italians when the ship was sinking. At that point in time, some whites called all dark-skinned people Italians regardless of their heritage. The superliner carried several people of color. Some came from the Middle East and the Far East.

Although the story about Leroy is fictitious, there is a report about stowaways that is associated with the *Titanic*. These stow-aways were Asian men who were traveling in second and third class. The Asians did not stow away on the *Titanic*. But they did get into a lifeboat without the permission of a ship's officer. The officer ordered the Asian men to get out, but they ignored the officer. It is possible that some of the Asians did not understand English. There are reports that an officer pointed a gun at the Asian men, but the officer did not shoot them, because he was afraid that he would accidentally shoot the ladies instead.

I wrote the first edition of this novel after reading more than one hundred books and articles about the *Titanic*. The few that mentioned people of color stated that blacks were not on the ship. Because the Laroche family remained silent for so long, this view was promoted in literature that was published as late as the beginning of the twenty-first century. I was not introduced to the Laroche's survivor story until I was revising this work.

In any event, the revelation did not change the structure of my story, which is framed around the behavior of first-class passengers. Many were prejudiced as revealed in statements made at the U.S. Senate hearings, the British government investigation into the disaster, and other records of the lives of the survivors.

In writing this work, I took very few liberties with the facts. This novel includes many little known pieces of information such as the fact that some people were seasick and remained in their rooms for most of the voyage, the interior of the *Titanic* was still under construction, the heat did not work some of the time, emergency drills were not done, there was a large rat population on the ship, etc. This novel also includes activities that occurred in the lifeboats and on the *Carpathia*. My story concludes with a view of New York City in 1912.

Many of the details about the ships and the lifeboats were obtained from oral histories and government hearings on the disaster. The facilities, cargo, animals, and even the food, were actually on the vessels. The captains were real. The other characters are fictitious, but with the exception of Leroy and Mark, their actions are based on activities that did occur.

With this emphasis on the facts, my decision to place a black person in first class has raised questions. Some people have provided answers that I never considered. Therefore, I think it is necessary to state why I wrote a black boy into the story.

It is a sincere effort to demonstrate that children are not born with prejudices. Unless young people choose to adopt the hostile and discriminatory behavior of some adults, they will otherwise find that it is possible to develop positive relationships with people of different backgrounds.

After all, everybody is *in the same boat.*

Wouldn't it be beautiful if we could all get along?

ABOUT THE AUTHOR

Corinne Brown has a Masters of Arts in history. She is a member of the <u>Society of Children Book Writers and Illustrators</u> and <u>Michigan Playwrights</u>. She has adapted *The Stowaway on The Titanic* into a play.

The author is also a poet. Her poem, *ABCs of Spirituality* list 26 simple acts one can do to enhance a spiritual life. This work, which is presented on a poster, is used as a motivational/inspirational tool in classrooms, offices, homes and churches.

The author is available to do readings, presentations and workshops for adults and children at libraries, book festivals, schools, churches and conferences.

Please visit the author's website by going to the site, writers.net and entering her name, Corinne Brown.

Or go directly to her homepage at—
http:/beta.hometown.aol.com/corinnehwkids/myhomepage/business.html

You may contact the author by email at <u>corinnehwkids@hotmail.com</u>.

ACKNOWLEDGEMENTS

My development in the writing craft is largely due to the faith and support of *Michigan Playwrights'* president and director, Sally Sawyer. For this, I am truly grateful. I would also like to mention my appreciation for the contributions of other members of *Michigan Playwrights*—Larry Altman, Mary Altman, Ann Forsaith, Gail Parrish and Sue Sack.

Many readers offered critiques that were of great value when the story was being revised. I am particularly grateful to members of the *Society of Children's Book Writers and Illustrators*, especially Kathleen Pranger, Christopher Paul Curtis and Esther Hershenhorn.

Cousin—Leonard Brown, parents—Mr. Dillon Brown and Mrs. Auvril Brown, brothers—Dillon and Dale Brown, sisters—Carolyn and Janet Brown, and friend—Rose Bruno, thank you for being early supporters of my writing career. A special thank you is sent to my nephew, Jordan Brown, who at age seven was the first person to read chapters of this book

In closing, the author expresses appreciation to Prof. Eugene R. Shaw, Ph.D. for conducting, free of charge, a final read through the manuscript. The author appreciates Dr. Shaw's efforts to give attention only to punctuation and grammar, and for respecting all other considerations as being expressions of the author's own writing style. Dr. Shaw is a professor of Education at Marygrove College, in Detroit, Michigan.

FREE DISCUSSION AND ACTIVITY GUIDE
available.
Email your request to:
corinnehwkids@hotmail.com

0-595-33154-8

Printed in the United States
39183LVS00006B/190-195

9 780595 331543